GUNPLAYIN' GREENHORN

The barkeep backed away and the place got mighty quiet when the kid almost sobbed, "I'm Jason Townsend, and I got my own rep as a man nobody had best mess with, hear?"

Longarm nodded soberly and said, "In that case, I'd rather buy you a beer than mess with you, Jason."

The kid said, "I don't drink with back-shooting sons of bitches." He moved fast, faster than most, as his gun hand swooped down on those side-draw ivory grips.

Then he was reeling along the bar with his cheap fancy gun still in its holster and two hundred grains of hot lead cooling off inside his ruptured but still-convulsing heart. . . .

DON'T MISS THESE
ALL-ACTION WESTERN SERIES
FROM THE BERKLEY PUBLISHING GROUP

THE GUNSMITH by J. R. Roberts
> Clint Adams was a legend among lawmen, outlaws, and ladies. They called him . . . the Gunsmith.

LONGARM by Tabor Evans
> The popular long-running series about U.S. Deputy Marshal Long—his life, his loves, his fight for justice.

LONE STAR by Wesley Ellis
> The blazing adventures of Jessica Starbuck and the martial arts master Ki. Over eight million copies in print.

SLOCUM by Jake Logan
> Today's longest-running action Western. John Slocum rides a deadly trail of hot blood and cold steel.

TABOR EVANS

LONGARM

AND THE APACHE PLUNDER

JOVE BOOKS, NEW YORK

LONGARM AND THE APACHE PLUNDER

A Jove Book / published by arrangement with
the author

PRINTING HISTORY
Jove edition / September 1994

ISBN: 0-515-11454-5

A JOVE BOOK®
Jove Books are published by The Berkley Publishing Group,
200 Madison Avenue, New York, New York 10016.
JOVE and the "J" design are trademarks
belonging to Jove Publications, Inc.

PRINTED IN THE UNITED STATES OF AMERICA

10 9 8 7 6 5 4 3 2 1

LONGARM

AND THE
APACHE PLUNDER

Chapter 1

A man had to study on his drinking money when he didn't have a job. But while the Parthenon Saloon, near the place he used to work, asked an extra nickel for a needled beer, it also offered the best free lunch in town. So the former Deputy U.S. Marshal Custis Long was down at that end of the bar, nursing a needled beer while eating pickled pigs' feet and potato salad, when his recent boss, Marshal Billy Vail, caught up with him.

The older and shorter Vail bellied up to the bar, snapped a German-silver badge upon the polished mahogany between them, and demanded in an injured tone, "What in blue blazes did I do or say, old son?"

Longarm, as he was better known away from the federal building he'd just stormed out of, coldly replied, "At the risk of sounding like your fool echo, you told me you wanted me to sneak down the other side of the Colorado–New Mexico line and ride herd on a heap of storm clouds hovering over La Mesa de los Viejos, which is ominously close to Jicarilla country."

Billy Vail nodded his balding bullet head. "I *thought* I said something to that effect just before you threw your badge

1

in my face and lit out like a schoolmarm seven unwashed sheepherders were out to screw."

Longarm washed down some potato salad with a carefully measured swallow of expensive beer and replied, "The government signed with the Jicarilla in ink after making them move twice before, speaking of screwing."

Vail seemed sincerely puzzled. "What in thunder do those Mountain Apache have to do with the chore I was assigning you when you went *loco en la cabeza* on me?"

Longarm sounded really disgusted as he replied. "The Jicarilla have kept the peace since '73. They have more in common with their Navaho cousins than they have with Victorio's mixed band of bronco Mescalero and Chiricahua. Yet the Great White Father, in his infinite wisdom, wants me scouting the hornet's nest he just heaved a rock through. I swear, the War Department must have dozens of congressmen's kids who just made second lieutenant and want that pretty red-and-blue campaign ribbon, even though so many Quill Indians have sued for peace. I suppose you hadn't read about the BIA fixing to move the Jicarilla down to Tularosa Canyon, eh?"

Vail shrugged. "Sure I read about it. I read everything. The powers that be feel the army will have a better handle on the really treacherous Mescalero Apache if they move 'em over to study war no more with their Chiricahua allies at San Carlos, under tighter rein from Fort Apache just next door."

When he saw he was getting no argument from Longarm about that, he continued with a bemused frown. "Moving the Mescalero out of Tularosa Canyon leaves an established BIA agency with nobody to agent for. So I reckon that's why they're fixing to move the far smaller Jicarilla nation south from that marginal mountain reserve and teach them real farming in—"

"Bullshit!" Longarm said, scowling like hell. "It's a pure and simple land grab! The Jicarilla gave us a hell of a

2

fight, surrendered under honorable terms, and were ceded barely more than a hundred square miles of mountain scenery nobody else had any use for at the time. But well-watered and half-timbered high country is still a far cry from the desert scrub the Mescalero keep running away from because there's no way even Na-déné could get by on hunting and food-gathering alone. That's what the folks we call Treacherous Apache call themselves, Na-déné."

Vail snorted, "Don't tell your granny how to suck eggs, or offer an ex–Texas Ranger lectures on Mister Lo, The Poor Indian. You won't get no argument from this child if you want to opine the U.S. Army has enough on its plate with Victorio and his bunch this summer. But you're wrong if you think I'd fib about Indians to any deputy who's been riding for me six or eight years. I don't know who told you the Mesa de los Viejos is within thirty miles of the Jicarilla agency at Dulce by crow, but—"

"*Now* who's teaching whose granny to suck eggs?" Longarm said with a thin smile. "It ain't as if New Mexico Territory is stuck to the back of the moon. How many times have we been asked to help the new territorial government clean up after the Santa Fe Ring left over from poor old Grant and his political bandits?"

Vail sighed. "'Political bandit' is a redundancy. I told you I read a heap. They call it a redundancy when you use two words to low-rate the same thing. Calling a politician a bandit is as needless as calling a woman of the town a whore, or an Apache an ornery Quill Indian. Man will cure the clap and fly to the moon before he ever gets the banditry out of politics. But speaking of bandits, I was trying to tell you about such shit down around La Mesa de los Viejos when you got all excited about your pet Apache."

"La Mesa de los Viejos ain't no thirty miles from that Jicarilla reserve!" Longarm stated. "I keep telling you I *know* that country. The hunting grounds those Indians signed for

3

in good faith straddle the Continental Divide down yonder. So Stinking Lake, a whole lot closer than Dulce Springs, lies inside the reservation line just a lope west from where you keep saying you want me scouting somebody *else*."

He bit a boiled egg in half, washed that part down, and insisted, "There ain't nobody else but Indians, dead or alive, up the canyons of that big slab of bedrock. They call it La Mesa de los Viejos because *Viejos* means 'Old Ones' in Spanish and the early Mexican *rancheros* were the first to notice all the cliff dwellings full of old dead Indians. Then they backed off to let the Old Ones be. Mexicans ain't as superstitious about dead bodies as Na-déné. Nobody could be. But anyone with a lick of sense could see they had no business settling canyonlands too mean for cliff-dwelling Indians to dwell in. Some Pueblo I know laugh at our professors who say the ancient cliff dwellers were from ancient Egypt or mayhaps Atlantis before they went extinct. The Zuni, Hopi, and such say their own ancestors started out in canyon strongholds before they just got numerous enough to move out on more sensible cornlands and hold bigger pueblos against all comers."

Vail nodded down at the deputy's badge that still lay on the bar between them. "I asked you not to lecture me about Mister Lo. If I gave a tinker's dam about abandoned cliff dwellings, I still wouldn't fathom how all this Indian bullshit has a thing to do with the situation Governor Wallace of New Mexico Territory asked us to look into for him. He asked for you by name, by the way. Seems you handed in the most impartial report on that Lincoln County war they were having a spell back."

Longarm tried some more pickled pigs' feet as old Ginger, the barmaid, shot them both a dirty look in passing. He told Vail, "You'd better order at least a schooner of draft, lest that sassy redhead reports us for taking unfair advantage of this free lunch."

Vail growled, "There's no such thing as a free lunch, and you've had your tantrum for the day, damn it. Those Mexicans you just mentioned have been growing their own corn and grazing stock along the Rio Chama, betwixt the Jicarilla you're so worried about and that mesa New Mexico is even more worried about. The established settlers in those parts report heaps of sinister strangers camped up many an old dry canyon, loaded for bear and reluctant as hell to tell anyone what they're doing there. Couple of locals have wound up drygulched, by a person or persons unknown. The closest thing they have to a full-time sheriff in such thinly populated country has declined the honor of riding anywhere near that mysterious mesa in search of answers. How do you like it so far? Like I said, they asked for you by name."

That redhead was hovering too close for Longarm to grab another egg without asking her to refill his empty schooner. So he nodded at her and held up two fingers as he told Billy Vail, "I can hazard a mighty educated guess without having to go all the way down to New Mexico. A land rush always attracts hired guns. There's one heap of timber and Lord knows what mineral rights to be fought over once the Jicarilla are moved south willing or otherwise."

"There ain't going to be any Indian fighting," said Vail in a dead-certain tone. As the barmaid slid two fresh beers across the mahogany at them Vail explained. "I told you I read. Things cross my desk you never see in the *Rocky Mountain News*. So I can assure you that me and Interior Secretary Schurz agree with you and General Sherman that the army can win all the medals it needs chasing Victorio and his glorified horse thieves to the south. The government's hoping your Jicarilla pals will move down to the Tularosa Agency without any serious fuss. The BIA is sending extra allotments and some Apache-talking agents to negotiate."

Longarm reached for another egg to go with his fresh beer as he said, "Nobody talks any lingo called Apache. Not their

5

Pueblo pals who first called 'em Apachu, meaning 'Enemies' in another lingo, nor the mixed bag of Na-déné speakers. They don't see why we divide 'em and dub 'em Navaho, Mescalero, Chiricahua, and such, by the way. They call themselves names such as Na-déné, N'dé, Déné, Tindé, Indé, and Lord knows what-all."

Billy Vail said something mighty dirty.

Longarm blandly continued. "The BIA might or might not be able to move the ones we call Jicarilla off that prime mountain real estate without a fight. Those not-so-mysterious strangers will doubtless get out of those dry canyons to the east and into the greener pastures of that big old reserve as soon as it seems halfway safe to plunder it. So why not wait and simply *ask* 'em who they are and where they came from, once they start filing homestead or mining claims? You got to tell the government things like that as soon as you file either."

The older man reached for his own beer as he wistfully replied, "I used to come up with easy answers before Sam Houston and me got nowhere trying to keep the Rangers on the winning side and I married up with a member of the unfair sex. If you and the ostrich bird would take your fool heads out of that Apache reserve and listen up, both that Indian land and the surrounding territory of New Mexico are the beeswax of the federal government, which don't want to wait for drygulching gunslicks to volunteer full confessions. Like I said, they asked for you by name. So can I wire Santa Fe you're on your way or not?"

Longarm told him to hold the thought as he headed back along the bar. Billy Vail had noticed the head barkeep sending that sassy little redhead into the back rooms with that tray, of course. Ginger was the sort of gal even a married man kept an eye on. But she was nowhere to be seen at the moment, and if Longarm meant to take a leak he didn't have to be so downright rude!

Then Vail saw Ginger coming back out with her empty tray, and sure enough, that tall, tanned drink of water was saying something that made her blush and cork him on one sleeve with her free little fist.

Then Ginger moved back behind the bar and Longarm ambled back to rejoin Vail, asking, "Are you sure you and General Sherman ain't out to tangle me up in Indian trouble just to wrangle a sneaky report on the poor Jicarilla out of me?"

Vail sniffed primly and declared, "I work for the Justice Department, not the War Department, and as far as me and Santa Fe can say, the only Indians up those spooky old canyons have been dead for quite a spell."

Longarm picked up his beer schooner to drain it as Vail asked again, "How about it? Are you riding for us or not?"

Longarm sighed, put down the empty schooner, and picked up his old silver badge to polish it some against the front of his tobacco-colored tweed vest. "Reckon I am. Lord knows I sure can use the money this weekend."

Vail smiled. "*Bueno*. I'll have Henry get right to work on your travel orders."

But Longarm quietly suggested, "Don't hurry old Henry just on my account, Boss. If I thought I'd be fixing to leave before Monday or Tuesday, I doubt I'd be needing *that* much money."

Chapter 2

It sure beat all how a gal could get off work on a Saturday as pretty as a picture and wind up so puffy-eyed and shrew-tongued on a cold gray Monday morning. But Longarm took her downstairs for a decent breakfast in the Tremont House dining room, and tried to be a sport as she counted the ways he'd used and abused her, all the while stuffing her face with pork sausage and waffles. A few cups of coffee later the little redhead had forgiven him and wanted to know if they'd be coming back to this same hotel when she got off work that evening. So he lost back all the ground he'd gained, and had to listen to some mighty unladylike remarks when he confessed that though it burned like fire, he had a train to catch.

He really did board the Durango combination later that same day. Old Henry, the priss who played the typewriter for Billy Vail, had naturally scheduled him to get off the D&RG Western at the town of Chama, New Mexico Territory, just south of the Colorado line near the headwaters of the Rio Chama. But Longarm figured others might be just as slick about train rides from Denver as old Henry. He had discovered to his sorrow that riders of the owlhoot trail tended to expect a federal deputy to be coming their way sooner or later if they were up to any serious sinning. So he stayed aboard to the next jerkwater stop at Dulce, where the tracks crossed one corner of the Jicarilla reserve.

This made sense in more ways than one, assuming his boss and Governor Lew Wallace were on the level with him about those mysterious gents a good day's ride to the southeast being white men the BIA didn't know from Adam's off-ox. For one thing, he was getting off where a lawman on his way to La Mesa de los Viejos had no call to get off. In addition, he was wearing a faded denim outfit instead of his usual three-piece suit and packing a stock saddle borrowed from the Diamond K near Denver instead of his usual army McClellan. And finally, a federal rider would be in better shape to dragoon himself some federal riding stock there without the whole world having to hear about it.

The D&RG Western locomotives stopped to fill up with boiler water at the Dulce Indian Agency because, as the Spanish name for the place would indicate, the springwater there ran sweeter there than anywhere else for miles around. But Longarm didn't care. As the train he'd gotten down from filled up on sweet water, he was already legging himself and his borrowed roper and saddlebags to the whitewashed agency complex, nestled between the broad, flat railroad right-of-way and the eroded cliffs of striped sedimentary rocks to the south. The higher peaks of the Continental Divide rose hazily to the east. Dulce already lay way above sea level, and while the Divide rose even higher, the mountains down this way, while still considered a stretch of the Rockies, didn't stick up quite as high as, say, the Front range west of Denver.

A brown-faced gent in a dark blue uniform came out of the Indian Police guardhouse as if to see what the tall, strange *pindah lickoyee*, or "white eyes," wanted. Sentimental reporters who paid a bit too much attention to that schoolmarm who claimed to have lived with the Lakota long enough to translate their bellyaching, wrote a heap of bull about the Indian Police being made up of trash whites instead of real Indians. Longarm knew the Indian Police were *run* by white men, just as the rest of the country was. But it would have been impractical as all get-out to have any police force staffed by underpaid white boys who didn't savvy the lingo of the folks they'd been armed and equipped to ride herd on.

Lots of Indians seemed anxious to join the Indian Police. Almost all their nations had traditional notions of warriors appointed to keep their own versions of law and order. And a chance to wear a quasi-military uniform and pack a gun had the more usual occupations, such as beating on drums and lining up for government handouts, beat by a country mile. So Longarm was surprised when the Jicarilla police sergeant strode over to stick out his hand like a white man expecting to shake like an equal, announcing in fair English, "I am Joseph Doli. I am a Christian. I am Nada of Those Who Make Everyone Behave at this agency. I welcome you if you come here in peace. If you are running away from your own kind, I think it would be better for us all if you got back on that train before it leaves."

Longarm said, "I ain't running away from anybody. But I ain't sure I want somebody to know I'm coming. Before we get into who I am and where I'm headed, might you know a *hatali* of your own kind known as Cho'chibas?"

The Indian nodded soberly and said, "Everyone has heard of that powerful medicine man, as you people say, *hatali*. What is Cho'chibas to you, White Eyes?"

Longarm modestly replied, "He calls me his Tsoi Bela-gana."

The somewhat older Indian blinked and let fly a whole string of rapid-fire Na-déné. So Longarm waved him down with his free hand and sheepishly admitted, "I don't speak your tongue and only savvy a few words at baby-talk speed.

10

Cho'chibas told me Tsoi Belagana meant something like 'American Grandchild,' right?"

Doli nodded. "*Belagana* is the more polite term we use for you people. It comes from the sound of American, not the funny eyes so many of you seem to have. What did you do to make a real person like Cho'chibas call you his grandchild?"

Longarm shrugged. "It wasn't all that much. I just ran off some other white eyes who were searching for yellow iron in one of your holy places. They had no right to be there. They were trespassing on reservation land your folks and mine had agreed on. So it only took a little pistol-whipping and—"

"You are the one called Belagana Hastin!" the Jicarilla said without hesitation. "The Nakaih call you Brazo Largo. Your own people call you Longarm. Have you come to do something about the trouble we are having here this summer? Our whited-eyed agent is getting ready to have supper with some others sent all the way from Washington, if you want to scold them for us."

Longarm shook his head morosely and replied, "I'd like to. But I don't have that much medicine and if the truth be known, I'd as soon not have too many others, your kind or mine, knowing more than they need to about my passing this way."

The Indian said, "I understand. I am a lawman too. I think you should come home with me for supper and we can talk about it where others need not worry about what we are saying."

Longarm said that sounded like a swell notion, and let the Indian steer him around the back of their guardhouse to what looked like a regulation BIA frame cabin, even though Sergeant Doli called it his *hogan*. The more famous Navaho *hogan* was a kind of home, which was what the word meant in Na-déné. Along the way, Doli told Longarm, not unkindly, that Jicarilla pronounced Na-déné somewhat closer to N'dé.

Only sometimes they said Tinneh, because nobody ever said their lingo was simple.

All the Indians Longarm had ever had supper with seemed to admire a haze of smoke instead of flies around them as they ate. Doli's moon-faced *asdza*—you never called her breed a squaw—had been expecting her *shasti* home for supper and whipped up a heap of *alta nabé*, the Jicarilla version of Irish stew, with blue corn substituting for the spuds, and juniper ashes instead of salt.

If they had any kids, she'd sent them out back so the two grown men could eat in peace. She served them generous bowls of her stew, and shyly asked Longarm if he wanted honey in his own coffee, but didn't sit down to table with them as her man waited for Longarm to dig in. So he did, and he was glad he'd been polite and accepted the strong but overly sweet coffee when he decided her juniper ash seasoning had to be an acquired taste.

Doli must have been more used to it, because he washed some down with his own ash-flavored coffee and asked Longarm if juniper grew along the rimrocks of that Tularosa Canyon to the south.

Longarm said truthfully he doubted there could be as much of anything green around Tularosa, but quickly added, "They do say the reserve at San Carlos is hotter and drier by far. It was moving old Victorio over to San Carlos that seems to have inspired his latest reservation jump. He kept bellyaching that he wanted to go back to the Tularosa Agency before he just went wild some more. So Tularosa has to be nicer than San Carlos, right?"

The Indian chewed sullenly, swallowed, and said, "An ant pile on a salt flat, covered with ashes, would be nicer than *San Carlos*! People who have run away from San Carlos have told us about the fine place our BIA chose for our Chiricahua cousins near Fort Apache. The land is too barren for the black goats of the Nakaih to graze. In the dry moons there is barely

12

water to drink and the children must go to bed with dust in their hair. The agent there told the people to plant crops, like Pueblo. But only greasewood and cactus grows well where it rains so seldom, and the hunting around San Carlos is poor, very poor. The people were asked to just bake there, under a crueler sun than they had known before, with nothing to do but get drunk and hit one another while they waited for another allotment. Can you blame a real man like the *hacké* you call Victorio for running away?"

Longarm didn't want to get into the distinctions between leaving a place you might not cotton to and raiding total strangers who'd had no idea you were coming. He said, "Be that as it may, nobody here at the Dulce Agency has been asked to go to San Carlos, and even if they had, I don't have any more say in the matter than you all. Counting on a fellow federal lawman's discretion, Sergeant, I've got orders to investigate other matters over by La Mesa de los Viejos on the far side of the Divide. Can you lend me some riding stock and have you or your local folks heard anything about what's been going on over on the far side of the mountains?"

The Indian said, "Choose any ponies in our police corral and they are your own from this day forward. I have heard nothing, nothing, about trouble around that distant mesa. It used to lie on Jicarilla range, or on range we disputed with others, at any rate. But now we hold nothing—nothing—much farther east than Stinking Lake. Once the medicine waters of the lake drain eastward toward the Rio Chama they are lost to us forever. Do you think it is right for Nakaih farmers to grow all that corn and squash with water they get from us without paying for it? Hear me, those Nakaih are not real farmers like the Zuni we used to have so much fun with. Like your own kind, the Nakaih came in from far away with their guns and iron tools to claim the best places for themselves. Why don't you white eyes make them go back to Mexico, where they belong?

13

Didn't you have a good fight with them, and didn't you win?"

Longarm smiled wearily and replied, "You'd be surprised how many white eyes might agree with you. But the peace treaty we signed at the end of the Mexican War gave Mexicans already settled in country taken from Mexico the right to hang on to their property and just go on acting natural, whether some of their new Anglo neighbors liked it or not."

The Indian scowled. "I have been told this before. But I still don't understand why Washington keeps that one old treaty with the Nakaih when it has broken so many—many— with *my* kind!"

Longarm was far more interested in that riding stock. But supper was still being served, in the form of a sweeter corn mush the lady of the house called *ta'nil'kan,* so he sighed and said, "Mexico, for all her faults, ain't never gone back on that treaty of '48. If she was to, say, grab Texas back or send her marines to raid the California gold fields, all bets would be off and we'd feel free to be mean as hell to the Mexicans or, as you call them, Nakaih."

"You treat us with scorn because we don't look as much like you as the Nakaih!" the Indian complained. "Hear me, we are men, not children! Why does the government keep treating us as if we were unruly children? Do we look like your white-eyed children?"

Longarm had to smile at the picture. Billy Vail back in Denver looked more like a big pink baby than the lady serving supper, and there was a hard black mountain gemstone called "Apache tears" with good reason. But since he'd been asked, he had to say, "It ain't that many Indians *look* like children, no offense. But you can't expect to be treated like responsible adults when you're living on handouts as wards of the state and are inclined to throw tantrums that would get a white schoolchild sent to reform school."

The Indian gaped at Longarm, turning a redder shade of brown as he took a deep breath, let it out, and said, "Your N'dé name fits you, Belagana Hastin. You *do* seem to be an American-people-have-to-listen-to. I know some of our young men like to steal horses. I am a police sergeant. But I don't think it is fair for you to say we live on charity, as if we had a choice. Hear me, back in our Shining Times, before you people came to change our world forever . . ."

"Spare me the violin music," Longarm said. "It ain't as if you and me are having a powwow on the shores of Old Virginee at this late date. You're an English-speaking government employee who wouldn't have made those stripes unless he could read a mite. So grow up and face the facts. I just told you why Mexican folks are allowed to just be themselves as long as they obey the same laws as the rest of us. Sometimes Mexicans steal horses. When they do they go to jail, or to the gallows in more than one Western state. But nobody sets aside reservations for Mexicans, or does a thing for them when they go broke through their own fault or just bad luck."

The Indian said, "That's different. They knew how to live more like the rest of you when they came up this way."

Longarm nodded. "Then try the recently freed colored folks on for size. They couldn't have been much more advanced than your average Indian when they were marched aboard slave ships and dumped on a strange shore to do chores they'd never heard of on their own side of the main ocean. You likely heard of the big fight we had over slavery and other differences. Some of the fighting took place out here, as close as Santa Fe. A heap of Indians got into it on one side or the other, or just raising hell in general whilst the army was too busy to ride herd on 'em."

The Jicarilla nodded soberly. "Your Eagle Chief Carson fought our Navaho kinsmen during that same war. I don't see what that had to do with the black white eyes getting loose."

15

Longarm said, "I doubt, if he was still around, Kit Carson could tell us. My point is that them colored folks *did* get loose, all at once, with no Bureau of African Affairs to treat them wisely or foolishly, and they were allowed to just sink or swim like everyone but you poor mistreated children of nature."

The Indian called him a son of a bitch in plain English.

Longarm smiled easily and replied, "Anglo folks, colored folks, Mex folks, and even self-supporting and law-abiding Indian folks are allowed to own property, sign contracts, and even vote in most states because they act like grown-ups and get *treated* like grown-ups. I know you Jicarilla feel the BIA ain't treating you fair right now. I said as much when I heard they were talking about moving you all again. I told you there was nothing I could do about it. But would you care for some friendly advice?"

The Indian said, "You are called the American-people-have-to-listen-to. How do you think we can stop the government from moving us down to the Tularosa Agency, Belagana Hastin?"

Longarm finished the last of his coffee, place a palm over his cup to keep his hostess from refilling it, and said, "Don't go. Get off the Great White Father's blanket and stand on your own two feet. Not the way Victorio has ridden. We both know *that* trail only leads to the dark world of the *chindi*. But you speak English. You can read it well enough to pass a sergeant's examination. That leaves you miles ahead of many a colored field hand who woke up one morning to find himself stuck with making his own living. I know dozens of gents around Denver, some of 'em working at good jobs for more than I make, who used to be Arapaho, Cheyenne, Ute, and such."

Doli grimaced. "I know others who have gone to Santa Fe to live off the blanket. Hear me, a lot of them are begging drunkards, or living off the quarters their wives and daughters make by selling themselves to white eyes!"

Longarm shrugged. "Men that worthless come in all shades from ivory to ebony. Always have. Always will. You asked me what any *real* man ought to do when he had the choice of running his own life or letting some pencil-pusher in Washington run it *for* him."

Doli pleaded, "Can't you at least talk to those government white eyes over at our agent's hogan right now? They might listen to another government man who knows this country so much better!"

Longarm sighed. "I would if I thought it would do you a lick of good. I'd try just for the hell of it if I wasn't trying to sneak into the Mesa de los Viejo canyonlands by way of a side entrance I hope nobody's watching. What if I was to stick to the high country most of the way, then ease through such cover as I can find, say, south of Stinking Lake?"

The Indian shrugged. "There is plenty of aspen, juniper, and pine along the ridges. You will find a high chaparral of pinyon and scrub oak as far east as the reservation line. I can't answer for the goat-loving Nakaih or cow-herding *pindah lickoyee* grazing right up to the line and sometimes crossing it. Nobody grazes the canyons the Anasazi used to dwell in. There is nothing there for a full-grown rabbit to eat."

Longarm nodded. "So I've been told. Yet others say all them strangers have moved in among them long-deserted cliff dwellings and seem to be guarding them from all comers. I'd sure like to know why. You say you had some riding stock to show me?"

The Indian rose from the table. "We have many fine ponies, many. Come. I will show you and you can have your pick. But I don't think you will find anyone over in those canyons you just spoke of. Not anyone *alive*. In our Shining Times, some of our hunters entered those dry canyons to see what might be there. Some came out excited,

17

to say they had seen *chindi*! Others never came out at all. The shades of dead people can be cruel, and a lot of people must have died when all those old empty ruins were still young!"

Chapter 3

Longarm rode out of the Dulce Agency just before sundown. He didn't see any Indians. That didn't mean a hundred or more pairs of dark sloe eyes weren't watching his every move. So whether it would be passed on or not, Longarm moved westward along the railroad tracks, as if headed on toward Durango for whatever white-eyed reason.

He was riding a black-and-white paint and leading a buckskin, seated astride a double-rigged roping saddle made by the Mullers. His denim duds, like his borrowed saddle, were meant to pass him off at any distance as a cowhand riding to or from some outfit not too far away. Most riders north of, say, Santa Fe telescoped hats of any color the same way because it would take a fancy Mexican chin strap to keep a high-crowned hat on when the mountain winds got frisky all of a sudden. Longarm had felt no call to change his sepia Stetson, which was overdue for some steaming and blocking in any case.

Despite the fool descriptions of him printed by reporter Crawford in the *Denver Post*, and despite the likelihood a lawman of some rep might be heading toward his real destination, Longarm knew lots of old cowhands sat tall in the saddle with a heavy mustache, and even more wore a double-action Colt on their left hip, cross-draw with the tailored hardwood grips forward, loaded with the same S&W .44-40 rounds as the Winchester '73 booted to the off side of the roping saddlc. He had iron rations for maybe three days on the trail packed hidden in the bedroll and personal saddlebags he'd lashed to the roping saddle's cordovan skirts. For when strangers rode by packing lots of trail supplies, a body could get curious as to just how far they'd come or how far they meant to go.

He'd left the well-broken-in manila throw-rope buckled to the off swell to add to the picture, since far more cowhands than lawmen rode as if they might be chasing cows.

It was an even-money bet he was wasting time and effort as he rode on into the golden sunset with the mountains he meant to ride over rising bloodred behind him in the lavender eastern sky. For it was one thing to swear a Jicarilla police sergeant to secrecy, and another to assume neither he nor his moon-faced wife would confide a bit to their own kith and kin.

But half a chance was better than none and well worth the taking when it wasn't costing more than a couple of extra hours on a cool clear-weather trail through pleasant scenery.

Though the gloaming light made it tougher to make out all the details, he could still see why the Jicarilla might not want to leave for any uncertain surroundings to the south. That fool report he'd read back in Denver said the BIA wanted to move the Jicarilla for their own good. The government was always moving Indians somewhere else as a way to improve their condition, and the Cherokee were still cussing Andrew Jackson for it after all these years. The report on the Jicarilla failed to mention the New Mexican cattle interests who'd cussed poor U. S. Grant for setting aside all this mountain greenery for Apache rascals who'd fought the New Mexico militia to a draw. Both Anglo and Mexican settlers had been fuming and fussing over all that swell range being wasted on fool Indians who didn't know how you made real money on marginal range and semiarid woodlands. The scenery along the way was too pretty for high country being managed for real money.

He was well out of sight from the Dulce Agency when he turned in the saddle to see a big fat star winking down at him from a purple sky. He kept riding away from it as he recited to his ponies:

> "Star light, star bright,
> Same star I saw last night.
> Wish I may, wish I might,
> See a different star some night."

Then he swung south, away from the track, saying aloud, "We'll see where this shallow dry wash leads us by moonrise. Ought to be able to circle Dulce and make her up around the eagle nests without too many Jicarilla spotting us in the moonlight. They don't find moonlight as romantic as us white eyes. They won't even go raiding after dark before they work up a powerful medicine against the evil eyes most folks call stars."

Longarm had more than one good reason to follow the southward-trending wash as darkness fell all around. The broad sandy bottom was easier for his eyes to make out, even as the steep, brush-rimmed banks on either side screened anyone moving along it. Best of all, since the snakes preferred twilight time for supper, neither the critters they hunted nor the diamondbacks themselves had any call to be scampering about in the open with two full-grown ponies crunching sand their way. High Apacheria got too cold for a sand-loving sidewinder on many a night, and the critters only bred where they could make it through the whole year.

Longarm figured they'd worked at least three miles south of the Dulce Agency when the big full moon popped up from behind the crags to the east as orange as a pumpkin ready for pie. So the next time they crossed a deer trail headed the right way, he reined in, changed mounts, and took it.

There was much to be said for mankind's way of laying trails the way men wanted to go and to hell with a few dips or rises. But riding a strange mount in unfamiliar territory, Longarm preferred to work his way along trails laid out by other four-legged critters. Deer, being in less of a hurry and having no call to work harder than they needed to, tended to wind along contour lines a man would have a tough time following even in better light. So neither pony gave him any trouble as they wound their way ever eastward with the light improving as the rising moon got whiter while appearing to be getting smaller. Longarm had won cow camp bets on that optical illusion. You proved your point by aiming at the moon, high and low, with a calibrated gunsight. It still *looked* all wrong, but measurement was measurement.

The Continental Divide wasn't always where the mountains rose highest. The uncertain dotted line on the map indicated where the falling rain wound up running down to sea level one way or the other. So while Longarm had to get over the official Continental Divide, it wasn't nearly as high in these parts as in the Sangre de Cristos on the far side of the upper Rio Grande. Geology courses wouldn't take four years if this old earth had been stuck together simply.

They still had some climbing to do before midnight and, deer not really caring which way the rivers might flow to the seas, they had to cut straighter and steeper as the rises got more serious. Few of the scattered crags and none of the passes rose above the timberline in this stretch of the Divide, but the juniper and pine thinned out to where the moonlight lit up plenty of open shortgrass, and Longarm was pleased to see they were making good time, considering he was riding strange ridges with no map but the more familiar stars up yonder.

It was a shame, or a blessing, that the folks called Apache had never yet learned to eat fish or admire stars. For mountain trout stuffed with onion-flavored blue-eyed grass and baked in 'dobe on the coals were fit to serve Queen Victoria, while the stars at this altitude made the black velvet sky seem spattered with diamond dust, at least where bigger fireflies weren't winking their asses down at you. It sure beat all how every nation seemed to pick some damned harmless thing to worry about. Pawnee just loved to stare up at the sky at night, and thought all the stars had names and medicines for anyone smart enough to ask the right star the right way. Most Indians looked at the stars the same as most whites. So why in thunder did the notorious night raiders of the Na-déné persuasion think moonlit or even starlit nights were so unlucky?

A couple of furlongs on a big fat star near the skyline winked out on him, and he reined in to reach thoughtfully for his saddle gun before he decided aloud, "Rocky outcrop on the next ridge. Ask a foolish question and Mother Nature just might answer. Of course you'd worry about stars giving your position away if you were running a ridge in search of harmful fun. But did the medicine men make up cautionary tales about evil stars just to make sure their young men raided on really overcast evenings?"

Mother Nature didn't answer. So he set the question aside, not being a fool Indian who had to worry about it. As gents reputed to delight in blood and slaughter—or maybe because they did study war so much—Na-déné speakers sure gave themselves a lot of things to worry about. Like the unrelated Cheyenne, the so-called Apache seemed to have a horror of death all out of proportion to their delight in dishing it out. Nobody mutilated fallen enemies worse than those two nations, because nobody was as worried about their victims coming back from the dead. Longarm could see a

23

certain logic in the otherwise spiteful practice of maiming and laming a fallen enemy after you'd killed him deader than a turd in a milk bucket. The Cheyenne admired cut-off bow or trigger fingers, while the Apache went for the eyes and feet. They called ghosts of any dead folks *chindi,* and just hated it when they met a *chindi* with its eyes and feet intact. For there was no way to kill somebody a second time, and how did you outrun or dodge a spook when it had its full power to play hide-and-seek with a poor mortal?

Longarm figured he'd made it over the Divide when they came on a streamlet purling toward the east in the moonlight. He reined in and let the ponies water themselves as he swapped saddles again. Then he took off his hat and belly-flopped in the stream-side sedge to water himself just upstream. Nothing from a canteen or even a pump ever tasted half that refreshing. He'd heard of a spring back East, may be in York State, where they bottled the water and sold it to rich folk in the cities like it was beer, for Gawd's sake. The odd notion made a tad more sense as he sipped such fine water after a spell of canteen water on the trail.

He sat up but didn't rise, seeing the Indian ponies were ground-rein-trained and seemed to be enjoying that lush sedge along the stream so much. He plucked a juicy green stem to chew. It tasted all right, but he felt he'd enjoy a smoke better. So he felt for a cheroot and his waterproof Mex matches as he sat up straighter, with the intent of lighting up before they moved on.

But he never did. Striking a match after dark in Apache country had been known to take years off a man's life, even when there *wasn't* somebody singing soft and sad in the middle distance!

Longarm put the cheroot and matches away as he eased to his feet. moved over to the ponies, and slid the Winchester out of its saddle boot. There was already a round in the chamber, adding up to sixteen if you counted the regular magazine load of fifteen. A Winchester '73 cranked sort of noisy, and that first vital round could ride fairly safe in the chamber with the hammer eased down to half-cock. He knew a pony trained not to drag its grounded reins could only be relied on to a point. So he quietly led the pair of them back upslope to a pine they'd passed earlier, and made certain neither would run off when or if it got noisier in those parts. Then he took a deep breath and cocked the hammer of his saddle gun all the way back as he eased in the general direction of that eerie singsong chant.

A friendly Na-déné singer he'd had fun with during a spell of ceremonial drumming had tried to explain the difference between the different "ways," or what he pictured as Indian psalms. But when you didn't savvy the lingo and the chanters only seemed to know one tune, they tended to sound a lot alike as well as sort of tedious. A Chinese gal he'd befriended out Frisco way had informed him just as certainly that she'd be switched with snakes if she could hear any difference between "Dixie" and "Marching Through Georgia." So it was likely all in the way your ears had been brought up.

He worked close enough to get a surer line on the direction that sad singing was coming from. It sounded like a gal, and she seemed to be sounding off in a spooky way, in that inky patch of juniper or whatever growing between two massive moonlit boulders. He felt no more desire to call out to her than he might have had moving in on any blind alley in Ciudad Juarez.

He'd read about this place where cruel-hearted gals called Sirens called out to passing strangers just to get them in an awful fix. So he had a better notion, and crabbed sideways to ease in on one blank wall of moonlit granite instead of sticking his paw smack in the bait pan. There was no practical way to scale the slightly sloping rock quietly with his Winchester. But that was one other good reason for packing a side arm. He placed his Winchester against the clean bare

25

rock and, leaving his six-gun holstered, he took a deep breath and went mountain-climbing.

He could hear the singing better as he scraped his denim-clad belly over the top. The words didn't make a lick more sense to him, of course. But the gal singing alone down there—he hoped she was alone—sure sounded hopeless and resigned as he slithered forward to peer over the edge at her.

He could see she stood alone, her hands up as if she was holding herself erect by gripping a sapling to either side. Longarm recalled the notorious Arapaho solution to caring for sick or elderly kin. He wasn't sure the Na-déné made a habit of abandoning old ladies to die of starvation if the wolves failed to get them first. It sure looked as if the poor old gal had been left all alone down there by *somebody*.

He let himself back down the outside surface, partly to give a white man on a mission time to think. He knew he'd never been sent all this way to play nursemaid to some sick old Jicarilla *asdza* her own medicine man had given up on. Such medicine men weren't all just rattles and dust-puffing. They cured sick Na-déné at least as often BIA surgeons did, and it sounded as if the old gal was resigned to becoming a *chindi* in the mighty near future. So there was no sensible reason for him to act like some fool Samaritan.

Then he had both feet on the ground. So he called himself a fool, picked up his carbine, and moved around to enter the cleft, trying to sound soothing, the way you talked to a critter, as he called out, "It's out of my way, ma'am. But I got a spare pony you can ride as I get you back to Dulce for some proper attention."

Then he almost shot the ghostly apparition staring at him with big black hollows as she pranced like hell, both arms held high and shouted, *"S's'suhah, Litcaiga Haltchin!"*

But Longarm only half believed in *chindis,* so he struck a wax-stemmed match and saw that what he'd been looking at was a stark naked gal, smeared with clay and wood ash, with a wrist tied to a springy aspen sapling to either side of her as she did a sort of barefoot Irish jig on a good-sized ants' nest. She must have seen what *he* was by the same flickering light, for she hissed in English, "Put the light out before they see it and you find yourself in the same sort of trouble!"

Longarm shook the match out and reached in his jeans for his penknife as he moved closer, warning, "Try not to bust the crust of the ant pile any more if you can, ma'am. I know the feeling. I've been nipped by red vinegar ants. But they only bite more if you rile them up."

He was sure she was cussing him sarcastically as he got to work on the rawhide thongs binding her wrists. He said soothingly, "Step atop my toes whilst I free you. The little buggers can't quite bite through that much leather, ma'am."

The naked Indian lady followed his suggestion, getting white ash all over the front of his denim as she plastered her naked body to his, a bare instep across each of his stout cavalry stovepipes. He wasn't sure he wanted to feel that way about a gal that spooky-looking. But he'd told her to do it. So he could only be a sport and cut both wrists free, even though she grabbed him like a long-lost lover with the first arm he got loose.

Then she was hugging him with both arms, and legs, as he backed off the ant pile with her, saying, "I got some aloe lotion amongst my possibles. Lucky for us both, red ants don't act as wild after dark as they can in daylight."

But she didn't seem to be listening. She'd already unwrapped her ash-plastered form from his to run bare-ass down the slope and belly-flop in that whitewater rill. The water was only inches deep and maybe a foot across. But she still managed a heap of splashing as she wallowed like an overheated pig set free in a mud puddle. She was already tougher to make out in the moonlight as she washed all that ash and clay from her saddle brown naked skin.

Longarm knew that, unlike true desert Indians such as Pima or the Paiute some called Diggers, Na-déné set more store in modest dress. So while she dunked herself in ice water from head to toe, he went over to the tethered ponies to break a Hudson Bay blanket out of his bedroll and a lead-foil tube of aloe-and-zinc ointment from a saddlebag.

As he ambled back to the naked *asdza* sitting upright in the rill with the moonlight glinting off her wet hair and hide, he told her, "You'd best get out and wrap yourself in this blanket before you catch cold, ma'am. I got some salve here I packed in case of burns. It ought to sooth them ant bites some."

She said she'd been stomping like that to kill as many of the red vinegar ants as she could while they were bedded down for the night inside that big mound. He didn't ask why. She allowed she had managed to get her bare feet and ankles nipped enough to matter. So he helped her out of the rill, wrapped her in the blanket, and sat her on the grassy slope to hunker down and rub salve all over her nether extremities as she told him her sad story.

She said her name was Kinipai and that her maternal uncle had been a powerful *hitali*, or medicine man. She swore four times she'd never lain with her own uncle, making it *so*, unless she was risking the wrath of all the spirits and holy ones by lying four times. When she said four times that neither she nor her uncle had even robbed the dead, he began to follow her drift. He'd been told by others that incest and grave-robbing were the first steps to *bahagi'ite*, or witchcraft.

Kinipai went on to explain how she'd been the victim of what a white man of the cloth might have called "a theological dispute." Her uncle had taught her many "ways" or chants before he'd been struck dead by a diamondback he was chanting with. It was thought a bit odd for women to take part in some of the way ceremonies, but it was not forbidden. So when they'd heard Little Big Eyes in Washington was sending white eyes to see whether the N'dé would have to move or be allowed to stay, Kinipai had decided to hold the Night Way, a mighty powerful ceremony. But older folks, best described as some sort of chanters' guild, had protested that everyone knew the Night Way was supposed to be held in wintertime, between the first freeze and greenup thaw. Then they'd argued that the Night Way was meant to cure the really sick, and only when all the other ways had failed and only strong *bishi* or dangerous spirit lore might save them.

But Kinipai had argued that their whole nation was on its deathbed and so they had to use strong medicine, without waiting for the right season. So she'd won out, for the time being.

Longarm could picture it, having sat in on such powwows in his own time. Indians could argue the finer points of religion and tradition with the fervor of preachers or lawyers debating, with neither a Good Book nor a law book to be found. Oral tradition depended entirely on human memory, and all humans tended to remember things the way they should have been, whether they'd been that way or not.

So Kinipai had held one Night Way, and then another, and the officials had still gotten off the D&RG Western to start working out the details of a mighty long walk.

They'd let her hold one more. When *that* hadn't set the white eyes packing, they'd drawn the line on a fourth mystical try. Failing four times was much worse, for some medicine reason. But as those vinegar ants had just found out, the small but strong-willed Kinipai could act determined as hell for a gal. So she'd put on her black-and-red paint, black for protection and red for victory—or sorcery, as some chanters believed—donned her black antlered mask, and picked up her basket drum and medicine stones to drive the white eyes away. She'd barely started before the others grabbed her and hauled her up the slopes to execute her the safe way. For the only thing her kind feared worse than a haunt was the haunt of a *witch*. It was likely to pop right out of her mouth the moment she was dead!

Longarm asked if the Indian Police knew anything about her being declared a witch. When Kinipai told him she'd been performing her Night Ways far upslope from any reservation settlement, he saw he could forget about reporting fellow officers and bade her to go on.

He had a better grasp on the unusual situation he'd just found her in when she explained how some wise old *hitali* had decided they could best avoid her *chindi* chasing them down the mountain in the dark by fixing it so she'd die after sunrise, after they were all holed up behind their prayer sticks and such. They'd bound her above that big ant pile, knowing the ants wouldn't really get to work on her naked flesh before the warm sun and some of her sweat inspired them to really buckle down. They'd smeared her with clay and wood ash to mask her protective paint and make her gray, the color of evil spirits and spooks. He had to allow she'd looked spooky as any *chindi* to him, over yonder in that cleft. He agreed with her that it seemed hardly likely that any of the witch hunters who'd left her to a slow agonizing death were likely to come back by moonlight. He already knew why you didn't start night fires in Apacheria, where a night watch was kept on every high point and the flare of a match could be made out at three miles when the moon clouded over.

He said, "That Hudson Bay blanket is four beaver skins' worth of thickness. I was planning to bed down on top of it, not under it, this time of the year. So I doubt you'll freeze, wrapped up in it till we can find you some more formal wear. How are your feet now?"

She said, "That was strong medicine you rubbed on them for me. I am too strong to scratch the bites and make them worse. Why have you been so good to me, Belagana? Are you an outlaw those *pindah lickoyee* are after too?"

Longarm said, "I hunt outlaws for the same Great Father. But I think he is wrong about you Jicarilla. Hear me. I have nothing to say about the move to the Tularosa Agency. I have been sent on other business. I was only passing through here on my way to La Mesa de los Viejos. My fight is with other white eyes, not your nation."

The Indian girl sat up straighter, eyes wide in the moonlight, and flatly warned him, "You will find neither your kind nor mine in the dry canyons of the Anasazi. Nothing lives there but the *chindi* of the long-dead Old Ones. Haven't you been told that the mere sight of a *chindi* will make a living person drop dead on the spot? That is why the *chindi* prowl the nights this side of the gray spirit world. They want to take us back there with them. They are lonely—lonely—in the ashen world of the dead because the grayness stretches out in many directions, forever, and one can never make it seem less empty!"

Longarm smiled thinly and said, "All in all I'd as soon take my chances with the limbo land the Papists tell of. I still got to get on over to that mesa and, seeing I got two ponies, is there anywheres I can drop you off where you might be safer?"

She sighed and said, "I have no place to go. I have nothing. The very clothes I wore this morning have been declared *ahidahagush* and burned to nothingness. I suppose I had better go on with you to take my chances with the *chindi* of the Old Ones. They could hardly be any crueler than my own people will be if they ever catch me!"

31

Chapter 4

In good times or bad it was best to travel at night and hole up by day in Apacheria, lest neighbors six or eight miles off gossip about your every move. So they watered the ponies good at a wider creek a ways down the eastern slope, and made day camp atop a pinyon-covered ridge beyond. For it was best to hole up on high ground, away from natural campsites, in Apacheria.

Pinyon was pine that grew about the size and shape of crab-apple trees, and offered fair cover and shade. Kinipai agreed that the many chewed-up scattered cones they saw meant none of her own folks harvested pine nuts along this ridge that often.

She was the one who spotted smoke-talk as Longarm was tethering the ponies deeper among the trees, with canteen water and cracked corn in their feed bags. Being Na-déné, she didn't call out to him. She joined him and the riding stock, silent as a shadow wrapped in a cream-and-black striped Hudson Bay. He'd been noticing for quite some time she had a pretty little face, by the standards of either race. For while different sorts admired somewhat different marks of beauty, everyone found regular features and a healthy young appearance pleasing.

She was letting some of her other charms show, now that her bare body had warmed up enough to feel a tad stuffy under that thick wool blanket. Jicarilla were more modest than Paiute, but not as worried as their Navaho cousins about unavoidable flashes of flesh.

He lost considerable interest in that one perky nipple when she calmly told him, "They already know I got away in the dark. They do not know about you helping me yet. If you mount up again and ride like the wind you may get away. If they catch you with me I don't think they will be as worried about your *chindi*. I'm afraid they will kill you faster on the spot."

As he followed her back through the trees, Longarm smiled dryly and said, "*You're* afraid? I've seen the carved-up remains of old boys your *hackés* had killed about as sudden as they felt like. But I reckon we'd best stick together for now, seeing you've got on my best blanket."

They were near the western edge of their pine-needle screen by then. So Kinipai pointed that way and told him to see for himself as she dropped the big blanket to the pinyon duff, revealing every bare inch of her short, firm, tawny body. He decided she'd likely wind up fat by the time she was thirty, but she sure curved swell at the moment. Then he saw she'd been asking him to look at the far-off puffs of white smoke hanging over the higher ridges to the west.

It wasn't true, as some whites thought, that Indians sent a sort of Morse code in smoke. To begin with, few Quill Indians knew how to read or write in any alphabet. Moreover, they didn't want strangers reading their mail. So they worked it more like white military men who agreed beforehand on passwords and countersigns. So many puffs in a row meant one thing or another that could change as the situation called for. Knowing this, Longarm wasn't too surprised when he asked Kinipai just what that smoke-talk said, and she told him she wasn't in that thick with the *hacké*, or warrior society, of her own nation.

He stared thoughtfully at the meaningless, drifting smoke puffs for a time. Then she hissed and said, "Over that way, to the north!"

He said, "I noticed," as they both stared in total ignorance at far more distant smoke rising from a higher crest in the morning sunlight.

He finally said, "When I cut you loose, that bare gravel betwixt the rocks had already been churned up by your prancing feet. After that, we both moved across green grass that'd had time to gather a new dusting of dew and spring backup by now."

She protested, "Those agency police ponies are shod. They will have left hoofprints, many hoofprints."

He nodded but said, "Not too near that cleft they'd left you in. And would you be tracking down even *Indian* lawmen if you'd just put a witch to death? How do you know they're chasing you? Mayhaps they're trying to get away. I don't know about you, but I'd be scared skinny if I tied up a wicked witch on an ant pile and came back the next morning to find her gone and the ants in dreadful shape!"

It didn't work. The frightened young gal threw herself against Longarm to bury her face in the front of his shirt and bawl, "I am not a wicked witch! I have no *bishi* to protect us! I have nothing—nothing—not even the medicine stones handed down from my poor old uncle, and how much *bishi* did he ever really have if that *tlick* he was dancing with could kill him with just one bite?"

Longarm held her soothingly. It seemed only natural to pat such a pretty bare buttock as he replied, "I'm sure it was a *big* snake, knowing how modest your medicine men act. I told you we'd get you some more duds to wear. And those scared folks who took you for the real thing ain't likely to assume

34

you've lost any powers you ever had, seeing they failed as full-fledged way-chanters to kill one pretty little thing."

She sniffed and said, "Thank you. I think you are pretty too. I wish we weren't going to die so soon. To purify myself for that Night Way I had to avoid womanly pleasures, even with my own hand, for four whole nights. Last night was the fifth and I was rubbing—rubbing—as I sat that pony bareback with its spine teasing me but never quite enough!"

Longarm got a better grip on her bare behind and snuggled her a bit closer as he replied in a desperately casual tone that *he* hadn't been getting any since leaving Denver.

So the next thing they knew they were down on that blanket, spread on springy pine needles, with her on top and bouncing up and down like a delighted kid on a merry-go-round while he was still shucking out of his duds. Like many an Indian or Mexican gal used to sleeping on floor pallets, Kinipai bounced with her haunches, with bare heels braced to either side of his hips as she braced her little palms against his hairy chest to slither up and down his beanpole in a delightful but sort of teasing way. So once he had his torso as bare as her own, with his jeans down around his booted ankles, he rolled on top to hook one elbow under either of her chunky brown knees and finish right.

She gasped that he was fixing to rupture her innards, but begged him not to stop seeing that they were both about to get killed in any case and this seemed a far nicer way to die.

After they'd both climaxed more than once and she found herself still alive and well, sharing a three-for-a-nickel cheroot with him as they lazed naked on the blanket in the shade, Kinipai giggled and confided, "I have never had anything that big in me, unless you want to count the time some of us were acting silly with corncobs when we were locked away to await the Pollen Dusting Way."

Longarm just chuckled and enjoyed another deep drag. He didn't need to be told how silly kids acted when they first found out why boys and girls had been built differently. Na-déné gals who'd started their first monthly period got locked up in a dark brush lodge to get over it together so their elders could throw them a fine dance and sprinkle them with corn, bean, squash, and tobacco pollen to make them strong and fertile women now that they were grown. Like the Pueblo they'd likely learned from, Na-déné set great store by pollen. It was never burnt as a sacrifice to the Holy Ones. To burn pollen was to destroy hope. But dusting a young gal's hair and making her sneeze with such powerful medicine was meant as one hell of an honor for her. It wasn't true Na-déné knowingly mistreated women. They just treated them unusually, by a white man's standards. It was usually Anglo or high-toned Mexican gals who went insane after they'd been captured by so-called Apache raiders.

Of course, all bets were off when dealing with a witch. So they'd barely smoked that cheroot down before Kinipai was nagging him some more about that smoke-talk. She'd doubtless learned, while learning English, how white eyes put up with much more nagging before they hit a grown woman. Hitting children for any reason was considered sort of unmanly by most Indians. But any Indian could see a grown woman had no call to carry on like some bawling baby.

Longarm told Kinipai so, adding firmly but not unkindly, "Whether they're looking for us or trying to get away from you, I doubt they have the least notion where we are right now."

She whimpered, "Hear me, my people are the best trackers this side of the gray spirit world and we were riding ponies, steel-shod ponies, all this way!"

He stretched out his free arm for another smoke, saw that his duds lay an unhandy distance away on the pinyon duff, and reached down to feel her up some more instead as he replied, "You're bragging a mite, no offense. Nobody tracks better

36

than Papigo, as some of your Chiricahua cousins learned to their sorrow a spell back."

He began to treat her friendlier down yonder as he added, "Don't ever stop running once you raid Papigo. They can track a sundial's shadow and cut its throat after sundown."

She reached down for his private parts as he assured her, "I'd be able to brag on scouting and being scouted by heaps of nations, including your own, if I hadn't been raised so modest. I made sure we rode across all the dry sod and slickrock I could find for us as we made her this far. We left that creek to cross gravel scree and mummified pine needles getting here."

She laughed and said, "This is crazy, crazy! We are playing with one another and carrying on a calm conversation at the same time!"

Having risen to the occasion some more, Longarm rolled his naked hips between her welcoming brown thighs and let her guide it in for him again as he grinned down at her and observed, "I know, and it sure seems friendly. I hardly ever go back for seconds with a pretty half-wit, but there's some gals I really enjoy talking to like this."

She hugged him down against her with her strong arms and chunky legs as he continued in the same tone. "There's this one old gal I know down Texas way and another up around Bitter Creek who both like to jaw with me about my work for the Justice Department. So every time I find myself that far afield, either direction from my home office, I seem to find myself having a conversation much like this one and . . . Never mind, that's two other stories, and right now I'm fixing to shoot my wad in a wicked witch!"

She bit down tight with her innards and pleaded with him to make it last and take her with him. So he tried his best, and managed to make it almost a mutual orgasm while they both made promises nobody born of mortal woman would ever be able to keep.

This time he really made it to his tobacco and matches. So as he sat on the blanket beside her lighting up, Kinipai sighed and told him, "I still say I would ride with you forever in the dark desert grayness of the dead. But there is a bare chance we could make it if we are not more than one good run from the reservation line to the east!"

Longarm took a drag on the cheroot and held it out to her as he said, "I know where we are. My kind ain't as afraid to look up at the stars as your kind, no offense. I've been studying on a downhill dash for the Chama Valley. You'd know better than me whether your *hackés* are sore enough to spill blood off their official reserve."

Kinipai took a luxurious drag to give herself time to consider. "I don't know. The BIA has my people very cross. Some of the younger *hackés* want to stand their ground and fight. But our older *nadas,* who have fought the blue sleeves already, think it may be better to move to Tularosa Canyon and live poorly than to give the *pindah lickoyee* the excuse to see we do not live anywhere forever."

Then she asked, "What has this to do with you and me? You are not N'dé and I have been banished as a witch, to be killed even slower!"

Longarm said, "Your kind as well as mine will suffer considerable if armed and dangerous so-called Apache make any reservation jumps whilst the BIA is meeting with their chiefs to discuss their future! I told you why I doubt anyone's hot on our trail. But sooner or later someone's sure to take you up on even one steel-shod hoofprint, and it might be best to leave him inside the reservation line as we work our way down past Stinking Lake. I told you why I have to work at least that far south. Others may or may not figure you're riding with me aboard a police pony. They're just as likely to dismiss any police pony tracks as the sign of a routine patrol by Sergeant Doli and his boys. Witch hunters with a guilty conscience might be a tad more interested in *avoiding* such patrols than *tracking* them. But in any case, once we're south of Stinking Lake, we can beeline for the haunted canyons of La Mesa de los Viejos, and what the hell, would you be tracking a wicked witch into *chindi* country if you believed in either witches or haunts that could kill you with a dirty look?"

She said she hoped he was right, but asked if they could screw at least one more time before they wound up as *chindis* themselves.

He was willing. Most men would have been. But he suggested they do it dog-style this time, so he could keep an eye on that smoke-talk from an upright kneeling position just in case.

She thought that was a grand notion, and gave him back his lit cheroot as she rolled over on her hands and knees. So he gripped the smoke between his grinning teeth and got a good grip on Kinipai's bare brown hips to pound her hard from behind in the cool ridgetop breeze. Meanwhile, off to the west, others were whipping wet blankets or deerskins on and off smoldering piles of green brush to dot the blue sky with white puffs.

He knew it would only upset the gal he was dog-styling if he told her there were *three* sets of smoke signals now. It unsettled *him* enough as he tried to read their meaning. The new smoke was rising more to the south, not too close, but in line with the very direction he'd been planning on heading as soon as it seemed safe to move out.

As she arched her spine to take him deeper, Kinipai moaned, "Hear me! I don't want them to kill you too. I think you should make a run for the Chama Valley alone. I do not think they would attack you if they saw you were not helping a condemned witch!"

To which Longarm could only reply, "Neither do I. But we get out of this together or nobody gets out at all, you pretty little thing."

Chapter 5

They spent the day smoking, screwing, eating canned beans and tomato preserves, but mostly talking. Longarm wound up learning more about Jicarilla medicine ways, or witchcraft, than he'd have ever bothered looking up in any library. But he listened tight because you just never knew when some bit of useless information could come in handy.

Kinipai confirmed what he'd already thought about the Jicarilla being as close to Navaho as the other official Apache nations. The Mexicans to begin with, and the Anglos coming afterwards, had accepted the Pueblo classification of Na-déné—speaking strangers who'd never known they were different nations. "Apache" came from the Pueblo word for any sort of enemy. The Jicarilla qualified as Apache by hunting and raiding a tad closer to the Zuni and Tanoan pueblos down the east slopes of the Continental Divide. "Navaho"— or "Navajo," the Mexican term came from the Pueblo word for a cornfield, *Navahu.* But none of the Na-déné involved gave a damn. The ones who were an inconvenient distance away for raiding corncribs had gotten captives to show them how to grow their own. The so-called Navaho had raided with almost as much glee until Kit Carson and the U.S. Cavalry, with some field artillery tagging along, had shown them the error of their ways back in '67. The Jicarilla had gone on raising hell as late as '73, making *them* Apache raiders instead of the domesticated Navaho. But Kinipai seemed to talk the same way about the same spirits as a friendly Navaho gal he'd met up with a spell back over in the Four Corners country. But when he allowed he'd heard that the Chiji, as they called Chiricahua, worshipped White-Painted Woman instead of the Navahos' Changing Woman, the condemned witch laughed and told him his kind wrote things down silly.

She explained, or tried to, that *neither* term was exactly what an Indian meant in evoking the friendly Holy One known to them as Asdza Nadle'hé, or Asdza Nadle'ché.

When he said both names sounded much the same to him, she smiled and said, "The Chiji speak with a different . . . accent? When white eyes with pencils come to put down the names of the Holy Ones on paper, my people try, but the words do not come out the same in English. I wish I could explain this better, but I can't, even though I have been taught both ways of speaking."

Longarm nodded. "I follow your drift. Sort of. A French Canadian once assured me the worst thing you can call somebody in French is a camel, a critter with a hump on its back and an evil disposition. But try as she might, and speaking English almost as good as me, she just couldn't say why it was dirtier to call a Frenchman a camel than, say, a dog or pig. She said those were insults too. But nothing to compare with 'camel.'"

Kinipai nodded. "When one of my people is so cross that killing would not be enough, he may say, '*Yil tsa hockali!*' And if anyone has one shred of honor, they must kill him for cursing them that dirty. Yet there is no way to translate the curse into English, Spanish, or even Zuni. You have to be N'dé and think N'dé to understand the terrible thing that's been said about you."

41

He nodded. "Son of a bitch loses a lot of its bite in Spanish too. We were talking about Changing Woman?"

She said, "Asdza Nadle'hé, oi Asdza Nadle'ché, is the mother of the Hero Twins who killed all those evil spirits, and sees that all things change as they should change, from birth to death. Her name can be written down in English as Changing Woman or White-Painted Woman if you change one sound a little. Our tongue is not easy for others to learn. *Your* tongue is as simple as baby talk. A pony is always called a pony, whether someone is riding it or not, whether it is in sight or off on the range somewhere. Do you wonder that sometimes we have a hard time explaining why we have to fight your people, whether you can see why we are cross with you or not?"

He had to admit his own kind had managed to get mighty cross with others speaking the same lingo. But that war he'd run off to once was water under the bridge now too. So along about noon, seeing those smoke signals didn't seem to be rising to the west anymore, he got dressed and carried the nose bags and his Winchester back down to the creek.

Nobody bothered him as he filled them and lugged them back upslope to the tethered ponies, while wishing they were mules. For though it wasn't too hot and dry that afternoon, horseflesh still needed far more water than either human beings or mules did.

As he was putting the nose bags back on the two ponies, Kinipai came over bare-ass to tell him it seemed dumb to take such chances. She said both brutes were N'dé ponies who didn't get watered as often as the fat pets of his kind.

He said, "I've an extra shirt in my saddlebags. We'd best see how it fits you if I'm not to spend the whole fool day with a hard-on. As to fat pet ponies, I'll tell you a dirty little secret of the U.S. Cav if you promise not to tell your treacherous Apache pals."

As she said with a sigh she had no friends among her own people, Longarm moved over to the grounded roping saddle to rustle up that pale blue workshirt, saying, "All that guff about noble Indian steeds in those Street and Smith dime novels by Ned Buntline is off the mark by a country mile. Us white eyes don't worry about stud books, horseshoes, and proper care because we're stupid. We *invented* horseback-riding, long before the first Indian ever saw the first horse on this side of the main ocean."

He handed her the shirt, and Kinipai put it on, saying, "Oh, this is so pretty, it is blue as the hair of Turquoise Woman. But hear me, I still say our ponies are tougher than your ponies!"

He showed her how to button up as he dryly observed, "Let's hope we can keep your boys from tangling on horse-back with those troopers at Fort Marcy, then. Your boys can hide amid the rimrocks just fine on their glorified billy goats. But no Indian pony can outrun a real horse on open ground. Do you know how many Pony Express riders the Indians ever caught up with between Omaha and Sacramento? None. Not a single sissy, oat-fed pony. The company lost one rider, arrowed in the back as he rode through an ambush. But his pony, and the mail, got through. It was the trancontinental telegraph that finished off the Pony Express. This Jicarilla riding stock I got off your agency police would make an army remount sergeant cry, but they're in better shape than your average grass-fed Indian pony. So if we baby 'em just a tad more, they might just save our lives in a running gunfight. You do know how to shoot a pistol, don't you?"

She sniffed and said of course. So he got out the double derringer he usually packed in his more formal tweed vest and unsnapped it from his watch chain, saying, "We'll have to figure some way for you to pack this. I know; we can use one of my spare socks as a sash, and you'll not only show less ass in that shirt when the wind blows, but you'll have a handy

43

place to pack a gun. Mind you don't lose it, and expect it to kick like a mule if you really have to fire it."

She seemed more delighted by that kind offer than by the magical blue shirt. He cinched her up, and when they found they could improvise a sort of holster from one toe and the hole in the sock's heel, he issued her some spare cartridges and showed her how to reload the simple two-shot belly gun.

Then, seeing how friendly all this had made her feel, they both took off all their duds to get friendlier on that blanket for quite a spell. They even managed some sleep, taking turns on guard. And then it was dark again and they ate more canned grub, watered their ponies and grazed them a mite nearer that creek, and mounted up to move on.

They followed the mostly north-and-south grain of the mountains, and made good time by moonlight. When the sun rose again they were south of Stinking Lake, after circling the fair-sized and not-all-that-smelly body of water in the wee small hours, when the Jicarilla camped around it had been trying to sleep and not listen to the owls all around.

Kinipai, being more educated than most of her kith and kin, was only scared, rather than terrified, whenever a screech owl cut loose in the timber they were riding through. Owl was one of the totems of Mister Death. When he asked Kinipai if she'd ever really heard any owl calling out somebody's name, she demurely replied, "Of course not. Only the person Owl is calling can hear Owl pronouncing his or her name. If I'd ever heard Owl calling *my* name, we wouldn't be talking about Owl like this. I'd be dead and you'd be talking to my *chindi*!"

Then she assured him that if ever she met up with him as a haunt she'd try to remember they'd been pals. She didn't know whether *chindi* gals got to spare old pals or not. She said she'd never been one or talked to one. He had to agree a *chindi* might not talk or think like a real live gal.

44

• • •

An owl who wouldn't quit as the sky pearled ever lighter led Longarm to a swell campsite in blackjack oaks on a rocky rise. But Kinipai didn't cotton to their avian neighbors at all.

The owl kept screeching because it had holed up for the day close to a crow rookery, and the crows were mobbing it with some mighty noisy remarks of their own. But when he explained the natural noises to the Jicarilla gal, she said Crow was almost as wicked a spirit as Owl. She naturally meant the "were-crow" ogre of her nation's religion. She knew the big black birds mobbing that real owl were only critters. But she said they still gave her the creeps as he insisted on making camp under nearby trees.

He told her that was the reason they were doing it. He figured none of her own folk would want to poke around close to owl or crows without an urgent reason, and he'd been careful about the path they'd been riding over slickrock and gravel.

By the time they'd tended the ponies and spread his bedroll upwind between two boulders, that owl had given up and flapped off to a quieter neighborhood with the crows calling insults after it. Longarm opened one of their last cans of beans as he asked an expert on the subject what she'd think if she heard an owl hooting in broad daylight with no crows as an excuse.

Her sloe eyes widened as she stammered, "I would run away, as fast as I was able, before I heard it call my name! Everyone knows only Real Owl could behave in a way Changing Woman hadn't meant all living things to act. Why are we talking about the Holy Ones? Don't you want to ravage me anymore?"

Longarm chuckled and said, "Let's eat first. I can give a fair imitation of an owl. You know how country boys fool around as they're growing up around critters. So what you're saying is that if I hooted at some Jicarilla heading this way to gather acorns or—"

"Nobody gathers the acorns of this sort of oak," she said with a wry expression. "They are bitter, bitter."

He said, "I know. Try some of these beans. My point is that I'd as soon not hurt or even swap harmless shots with any already peed-off Jicarilla during the current political crisis."

She dug into the beans with two fingers and handed the can back as he continued. "I don't want either of *us* getting killed by them, either. So any edge I can come up with might prove useful."

She washed down her beans with canteen water, and pointed out it was his grand notion to play tag with her people inside the reservation line.

He nodded and said, "I know where we are. Wasn't planning on a longer stay. We're almost due west of that mesa on the far side of the Rio Chama. One beeline after dark ought to see us there. I ain't sure you're socially presentable to the Mex settlers along the bottomlands between, no offense. It ain't that you look more Indian than a heap of Mestizo Mexicans, now that we've washed your pretty face. But I wish we had more seemly duds for you to wear. I'll allow that shirt of mine fits your bitty figure like a nightgown, but you still show a heap of leg on or off a pony. I wish I knew somebody in the Chama Valley well enough for a late-night visit and the loan of a more Mexican-looking outfit for you."

She scooped more beans from the can in turn as she thought hard and finally said, "I have a distant kinswoman who married a Nakaih she met off the reservation one time. It is the custom of our people to live near the bride's mother. But this one's mother would have nothing to do with a son-in-law who was not a real person, and for some reason he didn't wish to dwell among N'dé either. So they now live on a Nakaih *rancho,* where he works as a herder of the owner's cows."

Longarm washed down the last of their slim breakfast with the same canteen, and got out a smoke to share as he asked whether Kinipai's kinswoman was likely to know she was a condemned witch.

She said she doubted it, since that N'dé gal who'd married a Mexican had converted to the Papist Way and been written off as a lost soul by both her kin and the BIA. Indians who drew BIA allotments had to be numbered and listed on government rolls. Indians who went wild again after applying for BIA handouts were listed as renegades. But Indians who simply gave up acting either way and preferred to live as natural as anyone else were simply crossed off, as if they'd died.

As Longarm lit their cheroot the pretty Jicarilla allowed she'd hoped to enjoy a smoke with him *afterward*.

He told her, "We got a whole twelve hours or more to kill up here. It's best to study on other notions while you've got them on your mind. Might you know where this *rancho* your long-lost relation lives on might be?"

She said, "I've never been there, of course. But somebody told us it was too close to those old Anasazi ruins for comfort. I think they said they branded their cattle with a drawing of one of those big straw hats Nakaih wear. But it was upside down, like so."

He watched as she traced a fingernail in the dust between her upraised bare feet. He said, "That could be meant as a simplified sombero upside down, or a chongo-horned cow's head, right side up. Mexican brands are more artistic than our own."

She said that was the best she could do.

He said, "It has to be one or the other, and I speak enough Mexican to ask once we get down where it's safer to talk to folks on open range. Do you reckon your kinswoman's Mexican husband would take you in for a few days if we asked politely?"

The Na-déné gal looked sincerely puzzled. "What would *he* have to say about it? A man can *ask* his *asdza* to offer food and shelter to his own friends. But everyone knows she has the final say."

Then she scowled and demanded, "Why do you want to leave me alone among Nakaih strangers? I knew you were tired of me after all the nice things you said about my body! You men are all alike. You go through life like that wicked Holy One, Begochidi! You grab us poor trusting things by our privates when we least expect it, then you run away crying, *'Bego! Bego!'* as if you had done something brave!"

He handed her the cheroot. "Folks who say your kind and mine have nothing in common have surely never played slap-and-tickle with a lady of either persuasion. I ain't tired of screwing you, honey lamb. I just don't want to have to worry about another backside they might shoot at as I poke about those canyons on the far side of the Chama Valley. I told you why I'd been sent down this way to scout them, remember?"

The tawny little gal began to unbutton the front of his borrowed blue shirt as she lay back on the summer-cured grass between those rocks, replying mockingly, "I thought it was just to see *me*. Do you like what you see, Belagana Hastin?"

Most men would have, as she spread her chunky thighs wide in the dappled morning sunlight. For while all such sights were inspiring, some were prettier than others. She said she admired his dong too, when he dropped his jeans to show it was already hard.

So the day would have passed quite enjoyably, had they had just a tad more to eat as they screwed, smoked, and lazed the sunlit hours away. Then it was dark enough to move on, so they did, both ponies a bit balky now, and their own rumps feeling less rested than usual.

It was still fairly early after moonrise. So the other riders they heard first could have been on less pressing business than witch-hunting. But as the riders were moving past the cottonwood grove Longarm and the girl were hiding in, that blamed police buckskin neighed, inspiring the Indians in the middle distance to rein in and discuss the situation.

Longarm could only cock his Winchester and hope for the best for now. But Kinipai naturally understood what those old boys were saying about odd noises in the dark. So she suddenly let loose with what Longarm considered a rusty imitation of a great horned owl.

He said so with a chuckle as the Indians lit out at full gallop. When he told her she'd have never fooled any West-by-God-Virginia ridge-runners with such odd hootings, she demurely explained that she hadn't been trying to imitate *any* old owl. She said she'd heard one of them call another by name. So she'd wondered what they might do if Owl called out that name.

He laughed harder and said he'd always thought she was smart as a button. She sighed and said, "I've picked up some terrible habits since I met you. Pretending to be a Holy One is as bad as burning pollen. Our Pueblo enemies hold dance ways where masked elders act out the parts of their spirits. But I was taught by my uncle how disrespectful that would be to our own Holy Ones. I don't know how I shall ever be pure enough to conduct any blessing ways now!"

He said, "I don't see how, either. No offense, but ain't you in the position of one of those Salem witch women, if she'd got away and run off to live with the Mohegans or Pequoit?"

She didn't know what he was talking about. That didn't surprise him. He said, "I mean that, seeing you've been drummed out of your old chanters' guild as a tried and convicted witch, your best bet now would be a total change of position."

She said she liked some of the positions he'd taught her.

He laughed and said, "For Pete's sake, we're both dressed and on horseback. So pay attention. I've had this same conversation with a heap of disgruntled folks of various nations. I'm sorry as hell about that wrong turn Columbus took on his way to India, but he took it, and you folks wound up Indians, whether you wanted to be or not, at least as long as you kept on behaving like Indians."

She pouted. "Hear me, what is wrong with the way my N'dé people behave? We have always been this way, ever since Spider Woman showed us the way to these sunny lands from the dark caves we used to live in."

He said, "That ain't true. You own Changing Woman tells you that nothing stays the same, without changing, unless it's dead, and even the dead keep changing, sort of disgustingly, until nothing's left."

She said she wouldn't know about that, having been taught from her girlhood to avoid the dead and to speak about them as seldom as possible.

He shrugged and said, "I got to see more of dead boys in blue and gray at more than one battleground back East. So I see why a Jicarilla who didn't have to watch 'em bloat up and turn all sorts of ugly colors might not want to. My point was that *living* folks can cling to their old ways after their old ways don't work no more, or they can follow Changing Woman's advice and take up ways that *do* work. That kinswoman living Mexican on that ranch we're looking for ain't being asked to move clean down to the Tularosa Agency against her will. She's likely eating, drinking, sleeping, and so on as good or better than she ever did. And meanwhile, there's no BIA agent telling her to line up and sound off her allotment number."

Kinipai protested, "Hear me, she is no longer N'dé since she wed that stranger and accepted the strange ways of his cruel Holy Ones, the Mary Mother, who was not able to save her only son as Changing Woman saved the Hero Twins, and

50

the Jesus Chindi, whose medicine failed to protect him from his enemies and whom even his followers call a dead man's *chindi*!"

Longarm dryly observed, "'Holy Ghost' don't sound as spooky. I ain't out to convert an Apache witch to the Santa Fe, as the Mexican call their Holy Faith. I know this full-blood Arapaho family running a tolerable cattle spread up near Pikes Peak. Lord only knows who or what they pray to after dark. But in daylight they're taken for regular cattle folk with some Indian blood. Meanwhile nobody makes 'em fill out forms or sends the cavalry after them every time they order a beer after a hard day in the saddle."

She said, "I could never live like a *pindah lickoyee*! Could you learn to live like a N'dé if things were different and we were the ones who had won?"

Longarm shrugged. "I'd have to, wouldn't I? Given the choice of living as a grown man with longer hair and a different supper menu, or being kept as a sort of combination charity ward and museum exhibit, unless I aimed to run off and get shot up by the Fourth Na-déné Cav, I reckon I'd as soon adjust enough to get by."

Then he said, "It's up to you. I picked my race with more care before I let myself be born. Meanwhile we'd best get off the range of your superior kith and kin before they kill us both in some fine old traditional way you'd never want them to forsake."

She protested she didn't approve of *all* the customs of her own kind. Just the nicer beliefs, like Changing Woman, White-Shell Woman, or Rainbow Boy. She said she'd never be able to give up all her N'Dé ways.

Longarm said, "Let's ride. I'll teach you another way my own kind follow behind Queen Victoria's back. I reckon we could call it the Hypocrisy Way. Mighty strong medicine a heap of our own gals find mighty useful. I'm sure a paid-up witch could learn it in no time."

Chapter 6

Folks who didn't know many Mexicans with steady jobs tended to feel they were lazy because they took that long siesta in the heat of a sunny afternoon. Longarm knew they made up for La Siesta with a shorter spell of sleep at night. So he wasn't surprised when they rode down on a Mexican quartet stringing bobwire by the dawn's most early light. Their English-speaking boss didn't seem too delighted by the sight of an armed Anglo and obvious Apache coming at him off the Jicarilla reserve. But he'd been raised by a mama of quality. So he said, "*Buendias*. We are not stringing this drift wire too close to the reservation line, one hopes?"

Longarm agreed they were at least a couple of furlongs east of the line, and explained they were looking for a spread that branded with either an inverted sombero or a *cabeza de vaca chongo*.

The boss looked relieved, and said they'd guessed right with the cow-skull brand. He said they were looking for the Alvera spread, and gave them simple directions that made Longarm cuss under his breath. For while only a total shit would abandon such a sweet pal on foot with so far to walk, getting Kinipai to her literally distant kin was going to cost him almost a full day out of his way.

But pissing and moaning about that wasn't going to get them there any quicker, so he thanked the fence crew and rode on. Longarm had no call to ask them why they were stringing wire on public land. It would have only been rude to talk about reasons why no *vaquero* wanted to hunt for stray Mexican stock on Apache range with talk of an Apache uprising in the air.

Knowing the going would be easier up the east bank of the river because there'd be fewer side branches, they worked their way down to the fairly broad but mighty shallow Rio Chama to ford it.

Chama meant something like "brushwood" in Spanish, and Anglo settlers who liked to sound smart were quick to assume El Rio Chama had gotten such a name for the cottonwood, willow, and such along its floodplain. But in point of fact an ancient Spanish explorer named Francisco Chamuscado could have just as easily had that side branch of El Rio Grande named after his fool self. Greenhorns were always leaping to hasty conclusions about the West. That was why they were called greenhorns. After a dozen or more years out this way Longarm wasn't so certain he knew everything.

Once on the coach road up the far side, they had to ride the way they'd just come, inside the reservation line. Kinipai said she was sorry she hadn't known her kinswoman had settled that far north. He let her make it up to him during a trail break, off the trail in some tall rabbitbrush.

You saw far more rabbitbrush and wild mustard than bunchgrass and sage when riding up a valley grazed by beef stock instead of the deer the Jicarilla preferred to eat. As the alien but lush golden mustard gave way to more grease-wood and tumbleweed, Longarm knew they were within easy goatherding of some settlement. The Indian gal thought it was mighty spooky to see that much bare dust at that time of year.

They found the small but thriving trail town of Vado Seguro to be a cattle ford and market town used by both Anglo and Mexican settlers off the surrounding spreads. There were parts of Texas where you might see one breed refusing to drink with the other. But Anglos and Mexicans got along better in New Mexico Territory, having far more in common with each other than with the considerable Indian population, which ranged from hostile through barely civil, with none of them anxious to dance with your gal or vice versa.

Longarm didn't need the odd looks Kinipai was attracting as they rode in to inspire him to rein in near the market and buy her a frilly cotton blouse, a wraparound skirt of floral-print calico, and a pair of woven-leather *zapatas* to replace the moccasin boots she'd been stripped of. Her tough brown feet had about recovered from those ant bits by this time, and she seemed delighted as the elderly Mexican gal they'd bought them from showed her how to lace the *zapatas* to her trim ankles.

Longarm also bought her a small gilt cross on a fake golden chain. He wasn't just being a sport. Lots of folks, Anglo or Mexican, thought you could tell a Mex *señorita* of Indian blood from a plain old Indian by such tokens of La Santa Fe. Few of them knew how many Indians used the same cross as a medicine symbol, usually representing a star or the four mystical directions.

Kinipai had learned enough about outsider ways while learning English at a mission school she'd never wanted to go to, to grasp the symbolism of a cross with one leg a tad longer. She fussed at him while they were enjoying a warm sit-down meal of chili con carne and tamales near the livery, where he'd paid some kids to curry and water their ponies while they cooled off and ate some genuine oats as reward for a job half-done.

Seated at the blue-painted table under an awning, Kinipai

said she could see their colored waiter took her for a fairly prosperous Mexican gal with new shoes. But she said it made her feel funny, as if she was telling her own kind they weren't good enough to hang about with anymore.

He washed down some lava-stuffed tamale with strong black coffee and quietly observed, "It was them who decided *you* weren't the kind of gal they wanted blessing them the old-timey way, Kinipai. We live in changing times, as Miss Changing Woman warned you long ago. You can't go back to the Dulce Agency. They drummed you out of your old regiment under a sentence of death. It's as simple as that."

She protested, "This food tastes funny. These fine clothes you just bought me are pretty, pretty, but they are not the sort of clothes I am used to wearing, and I feel as if I am wearing my way-chanting mask, even though my face is naked, naked!"

Longarm smiled fondly and said, "Hold that thought until I can hire us a room here in town for La Siesta. I like you naked all over, and there's no sense pushing on through the heat of the day just to find everyone in bed when we get there."

She fluttered her lashes and said, "I like to get naked with you, even though you are not a real person. Do you think real people at some other agency would take me in if I went there instead of that *rancho* my cousin lives on?"

Longarm shrugged and said, "The Mescalero are fixing to get marched over to the Arizona Desert. The Chiricahua are as likely as your own Jicarilla to jump their reserve and give the army an excuse to scratch 'em off the government dole. I've spent enough time with your Navaho cousins to tell you they're as enthusiastic about hunting witches as the Jicarilla witch-hunters we just saved you from. So I'd say you had the choice betwixt conforming like a new recruit to the mighty strict traditions of strange Na-déné, or to the less strict Mexican ways. I understand from Papist pals that you can get along with a heap of fun as long as you don't rob the poor box or insult a priest to his face."

She had to smile at that picture, but insisted, "Hear me, I could never forsake Changing Woman, Rainbow Boy, or Child of the Waters for strange Holy Ones. Why do you white eyes make it so hard for us to go on living the way we were meant to live?"

To which Longarm dryly replied, "Meant to live how, by whom? I've told you I've had this dumb conversation before. There's as many ways to live Indian as there is to live white-eyed. Some of your kind may go on living much the same, with trading-post luxuries thrown in. A Woodland Cree trapping furs the way his granddad did has a lot in common with any other fur trapper, save for mayhaps being better at it than some of us."

He tried some more chili and continued. "The Pueblo farm folks you poor misunderstood Apache used to raid may be better off these days. My kind savvies any halfway sensible-acting cuss with a permanent address and irrigated croplands marked by boundaries anyone of goodwill can agree on. Your Navaho cousins have even managed to switch from raiding to sheepherding with some success. Their blankets, clay pottery, and coin-silver jewelry command fair prices at the trading posts, and it ain't as if anyone's asking them to pay rent or taxes as they find newer ways to live like . . . Indians, I reckon. I know they don't live like your kind or mine these days."

She curled her pretty lip and sneered, "Hear me, we real people no longer consider those sheepherding blanket sales-men N'dé!"

He said, "That's all right. The folks we call Navaho call themselves Déné. They think *your* ways are sort of dumb too. Can't you see none of the warrior-way nations can go on acting the way they used to? Nobody is pestering the Ojibwa as they go on gathering wild rice the same as ever. It's the swaggering horse thieves and buffalo hunters the Ojibway themselves named Nadowiesiu or Sioux that you see moping and weeping about the Shining Times they enjoyed at the expense of Ojibwa, Pawnee, and others raising crops instead of hair."

She sulked. "Hear me, my people never took scalps before your people taught them that trick."

Longarm snorted. "I know, it says in the Good Book how them Romans scalped Jesus, and everybody knows the English scalped Joan of Arc and anyone else they didn't like. King Henry scalped at least two wives, and the Spanish Inquisition was scalping folks right and left years after other Spaniards had been exploring on this side of the main ocean. Finish that coffee and wake up, girl. There's blame enough to go around. I'll allow some of our boys have been mean as hell if you'll admit nobody ever named your kind Apache because they came by in a sled giving presents to good little boys and girls."

To her credit, she seemed to study some on what he'd just said as they finished their plates and he ordered more coffee and some tuna pie. You made tuna pie with candied cactus fruit, not fish. Kinipai said she liked tuna pie, and allowed that at least some of her own kind had been a tad unreasonable of late. He asked her again if she thought the Jicarilla would jump the reserve or go quietly when the time came for them to move down to that Tularosa Agency.

She shrugged the brown shoulders partly exposed by her new Mexican blouse and said, "I hope those fools who wanted to kill me fight the blue sleeves. It will serve them right to be butchered by the medicine guns some say the blue sleeves have now. Have you heard about those medicine guns that piss bullets forever in a steady stream?"

Longarm nodded. "We call 'em Gatling guns. Custer was offered a battery of Gatlings to back his brag back in the summer of '76, but he was in too much of a hurry, or too proud. General Sherman will doubtless send mountain artillery into your Jicarilla mountain strongholds too, if push comes to shove. So if I was one of your chiefs I reckon I'd go along with old General Sherman."

She sighed. "That was why I was trying to chant another Night Way when they stopped me. The blue sleeves are too strong for us to fight. Victorio and those others who came out this summer are all going to be killed without gaining anything, anything. General Sherman is the one who said the only good Indian was a dead Indian, right?"

Longarm said, "That was General Sheridan. But you won't find him and old Billy Sherman in too much disagreement if he finds himself fighting extra Apache this summer. Finish your pie and let's go find us a place to resume our own hostilities, you good little Indian!"

Chapter 7

They made it to El Rancho Alvera by suppertime. It was just as well Kinipai had tasted more interesting Mexican food. For the tortillas and *refritos* whipped up by her former Jicarilla kinswoman had hardly any taste at all.

Despite the half-ass Mexican ways of their hefty older hostess, she greeted them both like long-lost Jicarilla kin, and the two gals babbled like brooks at high water in the melodious but odd lingo they'd been raised to speak.

Other Indians had assured Longarm nobody who hadn't been raised Na-déné would ever speak the language past the baby-talk level. Almost all the tongues spoken by the rest of the folks on the North American continent followed an entirely contrary grammar and general view of the world. So it was not surprising how much a keen observer could follow while, say, two Dutchmen, Greeks, or Shoshoni were talking. For most folks spoke with similar facial expressions and hand gestures that helped if you could pick out one word in a dozen.

Na-déné wasn't built that way. To begin with, as Kinipai had attempted to explain, a slight change of sound could turn a changing woman into a white-painted woman. And they did that with *all* their words, turning one thing into another with, say, an *m* instead of an *n*, or even worse, by using more than one word to describe what a white man, or most other Indians, would consider the same blamed thing. So just as you learned to call a coyote *ma'i*, some fool Na-déné gal would giggle and tell you you should have said "*atsé hacke*," and if you protested that that came out more like "first warrior" than "coyote," she'd look at you as if you'd just wet your jeans, and insist that everyone knew it meant coyote also.

In addition, their facial expressions and hand signals were just odd enough to make a stranger guess wrong about half the time. If the army ever had another war with the Apache, those Apache scouts working for the Signal Corps would doubtless come in handy. For nobody else could make an educated guess as to what in blue blazes the Apache had just yelled or signed down the line.

Ramon, the fat, easygoing Mexican married up with Kinipai's distant cousin, agreed that Apache gossip was a caution as he and Longarm jawed in Spanish over coffee and tobacco. Ramon seemed surprised that Longarm wasn't planning to stay the night, if not a month or more. But Longarm had no call to flash his badge and identification at anyone who hadn't asked to see either, and with good reason. So he let it go when Ramon said he'd heard a lot of Anglo gunhands seemed to be drifting in from all over down near La Mesa de los Viejos. When Longarm asked if anyone up this way had any notion what was going on down that way, the Mexican looked a tad uneasy and said he tried not to concern himself with matters that didn't concern him or his *raza*.

Longarm took advantage of a certain cooling off on the part of his host to say he had some riding to do and had best get it on down the road so he'd have a head start once the moon rose. Kinipai was the only one there who begged him to stay a while longer. She followed him outside so he could kiss her in the soft light of the gloaming and assure her he'd never in this world screw any other gal on this particular *rancho* should he ever pass this way again. He figured she was trying to make him feel possessive when she demurely mentioned that her Jicarilla kinswoman was out to fix her up with a *vaquero* who was three-quarters Indian. But it might have rubbed her the wrong way if he'd told her that sounded like her smartest move at the moment.

He went back over to the stable to find that, just as Ramon had promised, those two police ponies had been rubbed down, watered, and fed enough cracked corn to see them through the night and get them by for a day or more on such browse as he might find for them when he made day camp again.

But as he was saddling the paint, the tall drink of water in gray charro duds whom Longarm had already been introduced to as the *segundo,* or foreman of the spread, caught up with the slightly taller deputy to tell him he was wanted over at the *casa grande.*

Longarm nodded and let the *segundo* lead the way, aware how rude some might take his riding on and off the property without saying a word to El Patron in the flesh.

Don Hernan Alvera y Moreno was a severely friendly old gent with a gray spade beard. He was seated on his veranda in a wicker chair and a clean but rumpled white linen suit. He waved Longarm to another seat across a small marble table piled with *tapa* snacks and a pitcher of iced punch and got right to the point. "They told me you had ridden in with an Apache, wearing a double-action with tailored grips. If you are searching for work as . . . a man of action, I am prepared to pay five Yanqui dollars a day with private quarters and all you and your *mujer* Apache can eat."

Longarm smiled and accepted the tumbler of punch the older man poured for him as he said, "Miss Kinipai ain't my *mujer,* Don Hernan. We met up along the trail from Dulce, and I escorted her this far to visit with her own kin, La Señora Robles. As for my needing a job, I find your offer right handsome. But I've already made other plans and, no offense, I'd like to make her down by La Mesa de los Viejos by morning."

The old *ranchero* exchanged glances with his *segundo,* who said he had to get back to his own chores and drifted off in the tricky sunset light. Then Don Hernan said sadly, "I might have guessed you were one of *those* hombres."

Longarm put his tumbler back on the table and mildly asked what *those* hombres were supposed to be up to.

The dignified old Mexican looked as awkward as his *mestizo* cowhand with the Apache woman had looked. He shrugged and softly replied, "*Quien sabe?* It is best to vote the straight party ticket and not question Anglo political developments in Santa Fe, no?"

Longarm said, "I thought the Santa Fe Ring had been broken up by your new governor, General Wallace."

The old-timer cocked a bushy gray brow. "I am certain he can walk on water and raise the dead as well. They say he is an authority on La Biblia, and lesser miracles are more possible than breaking up that gang of . . . Never mind. You and your friends have nothing to fear from a harmless old greaser who simply wishes to be left in peace on mostly rocky barren range, eh?"

Longarm thought, then made a decision. "There's always going to be at least a modest courthouse gang around any administration elected by mortal voters. But surely the clique of lawmen, lawyers, and judges over in Santa Fe can't be getting away with the sort of things the earlier bunch under Grant got away with. I heard even U. S. Grant put down his booze and ordered an investigation after the New Mexico Guard sided with land-grabbers out to evict old land-grant families such as your own. Grant had his faults as a president, but he did fight in a war that was ended by that Treaty of Guadelupe Hidalgo, which said—"

"I know how the treaty conceding my own land to me reads!" the old Mexican said sharply, before adding in a dryer tone, "I was here as an hombre about your age at the time. *Es verdad* I have not been called upon to defend my family's land grant in court since your miraculous Lew Wallace replaced our . . . less formal Santa Fe machine. But those same guardsmen, along with federal troops, have taken sides in such discussions of land title as that Lincoln County War to the southeast, no?"

Longarm said, "No. Wallace offered a blanket pardon to all the gunslicks on both sides and sent in the troops to make sure nobody started up again. I know some say the McSween side got the short end of that stick. Others say it was dumb to go on fighting after a whole new crew of lawmen had been appointed with orders to throw cold water on both growly dogs. Be that as it may, despite some hurt feelings, Wallace ended the Lincoln County War once and for all, with both sides sincerely sorry they'd ever started it. You say you've had the same sort of bully-boy tactics up *this* way, Don Hernan?"

The *ranchero* shrugged. "I said nobody has tried to rob us with trumped-up charges that our title to this grant is mythical and hence open to more blue-eyed claimants under your Homestead Act of 1862. Perhaps now the politicos who concern themselves with such matters are selling chances for to steal land from the Indians. You know, of course, how much of northern New Mexico is still Indian land and . . . For why am I telling this to an Anglo who is no doubt laughing at an ignorant greaser, eh?"

Longarm said he hardly ever called gents he was drinking punch with greasers. But he got the impression his words were falling on deaf ears. So he repeated what he'd said about getting it on down the road, and nobody tried to stop him when he rose, excused himself, and ambled back across the swept-dirt central yard to the 'dobe stable.

There, finding himself alone with the riding stock, he finished saddling the paint and led both horses out under the purple sky to mount up and ride back the way he and Kinipai had come. Not even a cur dog saw him off.

A man could get the impression folks just didn't trust him, with Apache in an uncertain mood close by in one direction, and canyons full of other Anglo strangers up to Lord only knows what down the other way.

The ponies were rested and the balmy night was just right for man or beast. So he started out at a mile-eating trot, which was more comfortable for his mount than himself. Cavalry and cowhands trotted more than fashionable dudes hunting foxes. That was why both cavalry and stock saddles came with stirrups slung low enough for a rider to stand in and let the saddle hammer thin air instead of his balls while his pony bounced along at an easy trot.

He'd stocked up on more canned trail goods and tobacco earlier that day in Vado Seguro, so he had no call to ride back through the small trail town as he approached it some hours later by moonlight.

If there was one way for a stranger to be noticed in a small trail town, it would have to be riding in just as the card games and drinking had narrowed down to the regulars who'd known one another a spell. So Longarm circled the settlement through the hillside chaparral and rode on and then some, until he figured he was just south of where he and Kinipai had crossed the river much earlier.

He was already starting to feel wistful about the friendly little witch woman. But that wasn't why he reined in a furlong on. The paint he was riding was acting mighty odd under him.

Horseflesh wasn't made right for puking. A pony had to be sick as hell to even try to vomit, and when it tried, the little it could get up came out through its nostrils, which was dangerous as well as disgusting. Neither horses nor mules can breathe through their mouths. So what a man, a dog, or a cat would call a stuffed-up nose could be a fatal illness to a pony.

He reined off the riverside trail into stirrup-high rabbit-brush that for them horses to browse as he uncinched his borrowed stock saddle and put it aboard the buckskin, telling the paint he was sorry those Mexican kids back at Rancho Alvera had apparently allowed it to cool off too fast.

The paint just kept on retching, paying no attention to the brush that every critter that ate leaves seemed to admire. Then the buckskin lowered its head and started gagging too!

Longarm led them both back to the road afoot, intending to rest them both as the three of them strode along in the moonlight, with him mulling over all the agues and dyspepsias horseflesh was heir to.

They had plagues, the same as hogs and humans, but it was as odd to see two ponies take sick at the same time, within minutes of one another, as it would be to see two kids come down with the whooping cough while you were reading them a bedtime story. None of the other riding stock he'd seen since getting off the train at the Dulce Agency had looked at all out of sorts. So what in thunder could have gotten into them?

The buckskin, the one he'd thought in better shape, suddenly snorted odd-smelling vomit out both nostrils, tried to breathe in some more, and failing that, went into convulsions at the other end of the reins Longarm was holding.

That added up to a whole lot of contorted horseflesh, bucking and kicking and flopping about on the trail like a big dusty trout he'd hauled out of the nearby Rio Chama. In the meantime the paint busted loose, and might have run off if it hadn't been running in a series of circles until it ran head-on into a trailside oak and wound up flopping on its side like the poor buckskin.

Longarm let go of the reins, seeing they weren't doing a thing to control either brute. As the two of them kicked at nothing much and writhed like wiggle worms caught by the sunrise on flagstones, Longarm found some horse puke, hunkered down, and got some on one finger to sniff at.

Horse puke, like cow puke, smelled oddly sweet to the human nose. There was something in the way grazing critters digested vegetables that made the stuff smell like malted grain. But when Longarm held a flickering wax match near the vomit he could make out yellow corn, gray shreds of oat, and what looked like fine red pepper.

"Rat poison!" he suddenly declared out loud. At the same time the buckskin, who'd showed the effects last, suddenly went limp and just lay there in the moonlight like a big tawny beanbag.

Longarm drew his six-gun as he strode over to the writhing paint, saying, "I can imagine how you must feel, you poor brute." He dropped to one knee, placed the muzzle of his .44-40 in the hollow above the paint's left eye, and pulled the trigger.

He made sure the buckskin was as dead before he went about recovering both bridles, the saddle, and his heavy but necessary trail supplies, muttering, "They must have fed you ponies red squill by the sugar scoop back yonder!" Red squill is a weed used for rat poison by folks with kids and pets to worry about because it only makes a kid, a cat, or a dog puke like hell. Rodents, like ponies, can't throw up enough of the poison to save themselves. "I wonder which sneaky Mexican back yonder knew that much about ponies. There's no mystery as to who gave the order, or why!"

Tying the two bridles to the saddlehorn, Longarm hefted the heavy roper to one hip and morosely regarded the dead

66

ponies by the light of a silver moon. They both lay too close to the public thoroughfare. They'd spook hell out of any team or mounted pony coming up or down the valley day or night. But he didn't see how he could move either far enough to matter with just his one human back.

He got out a cheroot and lit up one-handed as he pondered his next move. He was a good way from that trail town, a sure place to hire or, if need be, buy more riding stock. Those Mexican riders he and Kinipai had seen stringing wire close to twenty-four hours back had surely been off some stock spread closer to that place where they'd crossed the river. Longarm decided it was worth trying a mile to the south, and trudged that way, muttering, "Don Hernan knew Ramon and at least two Apache gals might get steamed if he had his *segundo* drygulch an Anglo they were on good terms with. So thinking I was some hired gun out to join up with others, fixing to do Lord knows what down this same valley, he decided to just rat-poison my ponies and leave me afoot whilst they . . . what?"

Stranding a rider along the trail and making him walk for many a mile was a sure way to make him mad as hell, which was doubtless why the State of Colorado still hung horse thieves. It was run by old-timers who'd heard many a sad tale about long dusty strolls. But Don Hernan would have surely known his dirty joke would leave Longarm alive.

He shifted the awkward load to his other hip as he clenched his cheroot between bared teeth and growled, "Try her this way. He didn't want to kill a gringo close to home, but wanted him slowed down to an almost stationary target for later!"

That had worked, ominously well. Had he stopped in Vado Seguro the way most riders might have, those two ponies would have appeared to have taken sick and died on him while he was with the other Anglo riders in the saloon.

"Hold on," he warned himself. "Why couldn't you have simply gotten other riding stock at the town livery? Come to study on it, that town livery could have had rat poison of its own to spare. And you never told them stable hands in Vado Seguro just how far you and La Señorita might be riding. So gunslicks of either the Mexican or Anglo persuasion, coming up from them canyons after being sent for, could be expecting to catch up with you and Kinipai any time now and a considerable distance north of Rancho Alvera!"

He warned himself he could be playing chess while the other side was simply playing mumblety-peg like mean little kids who couldn't even say what made them so mean. For like many an Anglo rider, or for that matter many a Mexican, he'd strode through many a set of swinging doors to find himself in a whole heap of trouble with assholes who were just mean by nature and inclined to view a stranger of a different breed as a personal insult just because he was still standing up.

Longarm decided to set his suspicions to the back of the stove until he met up with a horse doctor who could hazard a guess as to how long it took to rat-poison a pony. For he was damned if *he* knew.

His load wasn't getting any lighter as he trudged on down the dark lonesome road, with night critters scattering off to either side as he made no effort to scuff quietly along the wagon ruts. A sneaky walker could get in a whole lot of trouble at snake time, the first few hours after sundown.

He was even more worried about spooking beef stock. His boots offered some protection from snakebite, but the undiluted Spanish longhorn was inclined to regard any human on foot as a target of opportunity, and while the moon was shining bright, many a shadow in the middle distance could well be a cow making up its mind to come tear-assing his way without warning. It was the female of the species that was more likely to really kill you, since the bulls tended to charge straighter and with their heads lower.

That was why Mexican matadors only fought bulls, and flat out refused to consider fighting even a bull of any Anglo dairy breed. They knew the graceful fawn-colored Jersey milker, both male and female, had killed more men, women, and children than all the other breeds combined.

He was glad most Mexicans drank goats' milk, and preferred not to think of the hogs they had ranging free for acorns, mesquite pods, and such. Hogs could be dangerous as well.

But when the strumming of a far-off guitar drew his eye to some pinpoints of lamplight way off to his left, he resisted the hankering to cut catty-corner through the waist-high mustard you always seemed to see around Spanish longhorns. The critters that admired the herb they'd crossed the main ocean with tended to lie down in it at night, and they could get up suddenly, with horns spanning seven feet from tip to tip, or nine feet if you measured around the curves.

He trudged on until, sure enough, he found a side lane heading to that isolated *rancho*. There was neither a fence nor cattle guard in evidence. So those hands stringing wire had been more worried about stock straying across the reservation line than goring poor wayfaring strangers on a public right-of-way.

Sneaking up on folks after dark could be as dangerous as the spooking of other critters. So, not wanting to waste ammunition, Longarm decided he'd best sing, out of tune, with that distant Mexican guitar.

It seemed to be trying for "La Paloma." So Longarm let fly with an old Irish ballad they'd based that trail song on. Instead of "Streets of Laredo," although to the same tune, he sang:

"Sure, pity the plight of a wayfaring stranger,
  With night coming on, and a long way from home."

It worked. He'd barely finished the first verse when that guitar ceased strumming and the lights ahead commenced to wink out. But the moonlit wagon ruts led him on through the darkness, as he switched to a more cheerful song about the Chisholm Trail, until a furlong or so on he heard a rifle cock and somebody called out, *"Quien es?"*

Longarm replied in Spanish, giving his true name but not his true occupation as he explained how two ponies had died along the coach road under him.

There was a low, urgent consultation. Then a feminine voice called out in passable English, "Might El Señor by any chance be the Custis Long some of my people call El Brazo Largo?"

Longarm, as that translated from the Spanish, sighed sheepishly and allowed he hadn't known he was that famous this far north of the border.

The woman called back more cheerfully, *"Bienvenido,* El Brazo Largo. You say you have need of *caballos*?"

Longarm said, "I'd be proud to pay for the hire of at least two, ma'am, and I sure wish someone might see fit to get the two I had off the road about a mile and a half north. I suspect they both ate rat poison, and in any case they're sure going to wind up somewhat disgusting."

He heard what seemed like a boss lady order someone else to gather a work detail for some hide salvage and an easier disposal than burial. Mex folks were as bad as his own when it came to letting folks downstream worry about their shit and garbage.

He didn't say anything. El Rio Chama ran fairly clear this far up, but it would carry the dead ponies into the far bigger Rio Grande, which ran as muddy and stinky as the Missouri by the time it got halfway to El Paso.

They'd made him welcome, so he moved forward, derringer palmed in his free hand, to be greeted like a long-lost rich uncle

70

and, of course, relieved of his load as the gal took his left elbow to tell him she was honored and that her *casa* was his *casa* for as long as he cared to own it.

He knew she was only being polite. Both her English and Spanish were spoken the way landholders who've never had to ask for a job were inclined to speak. He made out her retainers, doubtless armed, as eight to a dozen. Some of them had already scampered ahead, he felt sure, when he saw lamps being lit and heard more music up the road a piece.

By the time they got to the hollow square of 'dobe walls with red-tiled roofing, they'd established she was called Consuela Rosalinda Llamas y Valdez. He was sort of surprised, when she led him into her well-lit Spanish Baroque front parlor, to see that she was a Junoesque gal old enough to have a streak of silver in her black braided hair, and that she looked more Indian than full-blooded Kinipai had.

As she told him his saddle and possibles would be taken to his room, and sat him on a leather sofa near the glowing coals of her baronial fireplace, he recalled what that anthropology gal who'd kissed so nice had said about skulls. She'd said all babies had the same cute little bones behind their face meat, and that the kids of the different races slowly got more different as they grew up, with the outstanding differences waiting till they got older to stand out. He'd read about that sad case of the pretty quadroon passing herself off as pure white and marrying up with a proud and proddy planter, who'd shot her and then his own fool self when he just couldn't ignore the fact that his wife kept getting more colored-looking as they both got older.

It wouldn't have been polite to ask a lady with such a long Mexican name what Indian nation she might have hailed from way back when. That sweet-kissing expert on the subject had told him Na-déné were not as closely related to Comanche, Kiowa, and such as the Pueblos, who came in more than one breed. But although he'd noticed some

71

Indians were taller, shorter, prettier, or uglier than others, he'd learned not to make snap judgments. Indians tended to intermarry more than white breeds, being less inclined to brag about family trees. Some Mexican had obviously found Miss Consuela pretty enough to marry up with, wherever she'd come from. She was still a handsome old gal, and she hadn't learned such proud ways overnight. He decided she could have been a mission child. Before they'd been run off by the Mexican government, the Franciscan missionaries had done a tolerable job of turning Indian converts into fair imitations of regular Mexican farmers and artisans, which was why the Mexican government had put its foot down before Mexican politics could get even more complicated.

The lady of the house on a well-run Mexican *rancho* seldom had to give orders. Her willing workers had the mythical faithful darkies of the Dixie that never was beat by a furlong at anticipating wishes. So a pretty little thing with more white blood than his hostess had a big tray of *tapas* in front of Longarm in no time, with his choice of coffee or Madeira.

He allowed he'd go with the coffee, being too tired already for much wine. As she poured and served him, Consuela told him that, as he'd sort of suspected, she was the widow of an older grandee whose family had held this grant, close to twenty square sections, since way before that treaty of 1848. He didn't care. But as he was working on a *tapa* filled with mushrooms he sure hoped were safe, she brought up the constant bickering about land grants in more recent years.

Since she'd asked, he explained. "It's a matter of scale, ma'am. You know how much range it takes to raise stock in a land of a tad less rain, and I know from my own cow-herding days that you *rancheros* could use more because you raise stock Spanish-style. But the Homestead Act of '62 only allows an Anglo to claim a quarter section of land. That's twice the size of many a prosperous Pennsylvania

Dutchman's farm, but a pitiful joke in cattle country."

She protested that was hardly the fault of her and her local neighbors.

As he discovered a nicer *tapa* made with cheese, he washed it down with coffee, nodded, and said, "Nobody said it was, ma'am. The way Anglo cattlemen get around the restrictions of the Homestead Act is by claiming a prime spot for a home spread and grazing the unclaimed open range all around."

She shrugged and asked who was stopping them from raising their own beef any way they wanted. Longarm replied, "You land-grant *rancheros,* ma'am, along with the Indian reserves, I mean. New Mexico and Arizona territories, save for the state of Nevada, have way more land tied up privately or as reserved federal land than most anywhere else. The price of beef has gone up back East, as I hope you've discovered to your own pleasure. But even as cattle barons like old John Chisum are trying to expand, they run into Indian reservations bigger than some Eastern states, or privately owned land grants big enough to be counties at least. Your modest holdings wouldn't quite hold Manhattan Island, albeit Denver could fit in easy enough. But I can see how some new neighbor cut off from the river road by that much private property could feel vexed about the earlier administration's generosity. The Homestead Act came way after that Treaty of Guadalupe Hidalgo, you know."

She looked so worried he quickly added, "The real pressure in Santa Fe is for taking back all that land we gave to the Indians, now that we've found some use for it. I just came down from Dulce, and nobody I met was wearing war paint. So it seems more likely the government shifting all those Jicarilla will free up a mess of open range any time now."

She stared into the glowing embers of her fireplace, her own sloe eyes glowing back, as she murmured, "I know how most of your kind feel about the rights of Indians. I have, as you suggested, a new neighbor who would like to graze all

73

the way to the river. He has taken me to court twice since my Carlos died a little over a year and a half ago. He and his Anglo lawyers keep trying to prove I am an Indian, rather than a Mexican protected by that treaty, and hence, that I have no rights to this land now!"

Longarm grimaced and said, "I'm certain he'd just love to take it off your hands, ma'am. But you were married lawfully to the holder of a land grant recognized by Guadalupe Hidalgo, right?"

She said, "*Sí*, but alas, I was unable to give Carlos any children, and they say it was he, a *blanco* of pure Spanish blood, who held his family's grant from the old Spanish Crown."

Longarm polished off a pork-stuffed *tapa* and said, "I'm sure the court dismissed his plea because of the usual precedent's, ma'am. You call a ruling based on what earlier courts have found a precedent. That was decided years ago, out California way, when some earlier California Spanish raised the question in reverse. Seems this Scotch sea captain married a land-grant heiress who up and died, leaving a Spanish land grant to a pure gringo."

He sipped some coffee and added, "It was a federal court that held that inherited property was inherited property. They weren't about to hand over all that land to distant Mexican relations. You *have* been fighting off this rascal in a *federal* court, right?"

She nodded. "My own lawyers explained that to me. You were right about my being probated as the rightful heir to this land. But now they have raised the issue of, well, my being born a Zuni. I was raised a Christian by converted parents, but alas, I am afraid I have pure Indian blood!"

Longarm shrugged. "That has to have *impure* blood of any sort beat. I got to ask you a mighty personal question if I'm to go on, ma'am. I ain't asking for exact figures, but is it safe to say you were born the other side of 1848?"

She dimpled and said, "Of course I was, you flatterer. But what difference might my age make? An Indian is an Indian, no?"

He said, "No. Under Mexican laws, left over from the Spanish, a Spanish-speaking Christian who wore shoes and got a haircut now and again was a full citizen with all the rights of any other Spanish subject or law abiding Mexican under the republic. You do pay taxes on this *rancho,* don't you?"

She nodded, but said, "Those Anglo lawyers say that only proves how primitive I am, because Indians are not required to pay taxes on their lands under your laws. But my lawyers tell me they think I should go on paying my land taxes anyway."

Longarm nodded. "You've got the right lawyers, Miss Consuela. You and your folks living Christian, apart from other Zuni, if I know my Pueblo medicine men, means you were never listed as any sort of Indians by the Bureau of Indian Affairs, right?"

She nodded. "My parents were working for the parents of my poor Carlos when Mexico lost that war with your people. Nobody ever asked us what we were until most recently. But they say I am still an Indian and that the U.S. Constitution gives no rights to Indians. They showed me the paragraph, in black and white. I cried. It seemed so cruel and unjust!"

He said, "It would be, if that was the way it read. But you missed the details, Miss Consuela. What may appear to exclude Indians from the Bill of Rights reads, 'Indians not taxed.' It don't read Indians in general as a race. Shucks, colored folks and even Swedes are fully protected by the Bill of Rights since the war, at least as far as *federal* law extends, and New Mexico is a federal territory."

She said she didn't understand. A lot of well-meaning folks didn't.

He explained. "When the Founding Fathers drew up the Constitution, they naturally had to deal with the simple fact that heaps of Quill Indians were still lurking in the woods all the way back East. So they divided Indians up into folks like the Christian Stockbridges, a mess of Mohegans who'd fought on our side at Bunker Hill, and the wilder sorts, such as Mohawk and Shawnee, who'd traded Yankee scalps for firewater from Hair-Buying Hamilton, the royal governor up to Detroit."

She sniffed. "In other words, they divided Indians into those they thought tame and those they thought wild?"

He said, "Sure. It would have been dumb to divide them any other way. The real point is that even then there were Indians acting like everyone else and, well, folks who had to be dealt with differently. So what that clause about untaxed Indians really means is that nobody can expect to have the full rights of an adult citizen as long as they're off the tax rolls, as public charges or wards of the state."

He tried another *tapa*, decided he'd best quit while he was ahead, and added, "Wouldn't make much sense to let men vote whilst they were at war with the government, either. So whilst Victorio or even one of those reservation Jicarilla would have a tough time voting in the next election, that clause about Indians can't apply to *you*. Anyone who pays taxes on property lawfully come by is by definition a tax-paying property-holder, be she white, red, or a becoming shade of lavender. I have this argument all the time with boys who've been led to believe only their kind have any rights. Not all such pains in the neck are white, by the way."

She laughed and said she'd heard Victorio could be awfully bossy. Then she asked him if he was ready for bed. He'd been ready for bed since first he'd noticed how she filled out that white blouse and cordovan riding skirt. But when he said that sounded like a mighty fine notion, she tinkled a small brass bell and that same serving gal came in to show their honored guest to his room for the night.

She led the way out back and along a long archway, holding up a candle they really didn't need until they got there. The cell-like room, furnished with a four-poster bed and an oaken wardrobe, was a bit severe but smelled of rosewater. He saw, when the *chica* put the candlestick on a small bedtable, that the 'dobe walls had been recently replastered.

Then he saw the pretty little Mex gal was crying, too, although she was trying not to show it as she shut the door, shot the bolt, and moved over by the bed to start shucking her duds.

It didn't take a gal starting out with just a blouse and skirt too long to undress. He had to admire what she had to show a man as she stood there resigned, crying fit to bust.

Longarm spotted his borrowed saddle and possibles, including his Winchester, in the corner on the far side of the four-poster. He took off no more than his own hat as he quietly asked her in Spanish what her *patrona* had told her about him.

The *chica* licked her lips and replied in a trembling voice that all she knew was that it would be a great honor to spend the night with such a distinguished guest.

Longarm stayed on his side of the room as he quietly questioned her to find out if she usually obeyed her boss lady of her own free will, or whether a federal law covering peonage as well as chattel slavery might be getting all bent out of shape.

He worded his questions carefully. The mean thing about peonage was that, unlike outright slavery, it was tougher for even its own victims to define. There was a mighty fine line between slavery and peonage, or what they called "the patron system." Many an Anglo boss asked his workers to do things they didn't want to. Such power went with being the boss. But peonage went over the line by allowing the services, if not the flesh and blood, of a servant bound by debt to be bought and sold.

But as he questioned the naked and increasingly less frightened young gal, it developed that Miss Consuela had sent word back to her kitchen that whichever serving gal might volunteer to take care of El Brazo Largo would have the next two days off with pay.

Longarm chuckled as he imagined the scene in the kitchen, and asked why she'd volunteered if she was so scared.

She said she wasn't scared of *him.* She was afraid her *querido,* a handsome young *vaquero,* would be jealous. She said it had seemed like a swell way to buy the extra time alone with her Pablo, before she had taken time to consider how Pablo might feel about it.

Longarm was thinking about jealous young *vaqueros* himself as he gently suggested, "I've had a very tiring day. Maybe it would be better if you just got dressed and we forgot all about this, eh?"

She brightened, but said, "The others will still tell Pablo that I gave myself to a gringo, no?"

He said, "Not if you go right to him from here. There's no good reason to tell the whole *rancho* where you spent the night, is there?"

She scooped up her duds from the floor, gushing, "Oh, they were right about you being most *simpatico* for a gringo! You are certain you do not feel scorned? You shall not suffer later?"

He assured her they were parting friends. So she got dressed almost as fast as she'd stripped, and then hesitated before leaving, saying she might manage a quick one, lest he think she thought him repulsive.

But he sent her on her way to bed down with her heart's desire and maybe save himself more trouble. Old Consuela, despite her obvious desire to please, had made it clear his kind wasn't all that popular in these parts.

Chapter 8

Longarm felt a tad awkward at breakfast. It was ample, and served alfresco on the shady side of the main house while the morning air still tasted tangy. He was served alone at the table with the dusky lady of the house. He saw she'd changed into a black lace outfit that was likely cooler than her riding duds of the night before. Being richer than some of her own kith and kin, she ate a bit more Anglo, which is to say she ate better grub cooked more plainly. Longarm had noticed that all the really elaborate styles of cooking from Chinese to Hungarian had been invented by people who had to stretch the more expensive cuts, and spice tasteless filling up with fancy flavoring. That was likely why rich folks asked for rare steak and railroad workers fancied corned beef. You could eat a tender T-bone close to the way it came off the cow, but you needed to marinate cheaper and tougher chuck in tasty pickle liquor for a spell before you could bite into it.

Consuela Llamas fed him scrambled eggs and acorn-fed ham from her own swine herd, along with coffee strong enough to strip paint. He'd been worried about free-ranging hogs the night before, knowing how Mexican *rancheros* grazed more kinds of critters, from cows to poultry, than most Anglo stockmen.

Longarm knew why old Consuela was smiling like old Mona Lisa as she asked him if he'd had a comfortable night. He managed to meet her gaze with a poker face as he allowed he'd had no complaints. It was up to the ladies to say whether they'd been pure as the driven snow or had taken it all three ways more than once. He'd always thought that Casanova had been a fool, if not a liar, spelling out just when and where he'd played slap-and-tickle and the exact number of gals he'd played it with. For few believed a braggart to begin with. And the ones who'd bought your brag might hear of some other great lover who'd scored higher. So Longarm was sure his considerable rep as a horny Denver devil stemmed from the simple fact that nobody in town could say for certain *who* he might or might not have slept with in such a good-sized town.

Then Consuela calmly asked him what he'd found distasteful about poor Ynez.

He wrinkled his nose and replied that if Ynez had been the handle of that lady who'd led his way to bed, he'd found her tolerable to look at. "I haven't asked who *you* found repulsive last night, or vice versa, because to tell the truth I'm more worried about that John Brown, the head butler they say Queen Victoria may be carrying on with. The picture's a mite more amusing, no offense. *Nice*-looking folks all look about the same in bed together."

She blushed a deeper shade of chestnut as she softly said she was sorry if she'd offended him. Then she chuckled and said she saw what he meant, that she'd laughed like hell the first time she'd pictured the fat Prince of Wales atop his skinny redheaded princess from Denmark.

Longarm didn't say he'd heard Prince Edward had been going at it hot and heavy with Miss Lillie Langtry, that actress gal, because for one thing he wasn't certain it was true, and for another he had to get on down the road. So he mentioned horseflesh instead and she said she was sorry about him having to bring that up.

They finished their coffee. He expected to follow her around to the corrals to look over her remuda, but she tinkled that same bell—it seemed to follow her about like a brass pup—and when yet another servant gal came out on the veranda, Consuela told her they wanted to see eight ponies which she reeled off by name. Then she gave Longarm permission to smoke and allowed she'd try one of his skinny cheroots herself.

A short spell later, four of her *vaqueros* herded what she called her eight best ponies around a corner through the wild mustard and green tumbleweed. Longarm had to take part of what she said on faith, but he decided any horseflesh she was holding back on had to be the queen bee's knees. All eight ponies were cream to palomino Spanish barbs, that beauteous cross between Arab ponies from the Barbary Coast of North Africa and the bigger and steadier chargers old-time Spanish fighting men like those El Cid had favored. Consuela said her late husband had been a big man. Longarm believed her when he saw that not one of those ponies stood less than fifteen hands at the shoulder despite their flaring nostrils and intelligent spaniel eyes. Those bright hunting dogs, as their name still hinted, were another old Spanish notion. Spanish-speaking folks bred critters as cleverly as French-speaking folks pruned grape vines for wine.

Longarm allowed he'd settle for the two with the longer limbs, a palomino gelding and a more African-looking mare the color of that rich cream you get from a Guernsey milker. He said he was more intent on covering distance than cutting cows in chaparral, and she said she admired a man who knew just what he wanted.

She told her *segundo,* one of those riders he'd seen stringing wire while riding with Kinipai, to bridle both brutes, and asked Longarm which one he wanted to start out on. He said he fancied a ride on that white mare, and she told her boys to get cracking and bring the stock right back ready to go. So they did.

He and Consuela had time to jaw just a bit about her troubles and his plans. He tried to stay on the topic of her pestiferous Anglo neighbors. Not because he really expected to do anything about them, but because he didn't want to say just where he'd be headed next. It was bad enough she knew who he was. He'd told her he was on a secret job and sworn her to silence, but the less she knew the better.

When two of her riders led the stock he'd picked back again, all set up to go, he got an idea how well she meant to keep his secret. For when he brought up the delicate subject of money again, she protested that he was a guest, and added something about the value of being known for having supplied two *caballos* to El Brazo Largo.

It wouldn't have been polite to cuss her, or useful to warn her again not to gossip about him. So he just mounted the cream, took the lead of the palomino with a nod of thanks, and rode out.

With the sun up and nobody likely to be laying for him in the high weeds, Longarm headed for the coach road catty-corner through the stirrup-deep wild mustard. The air was still crisp and the tang of tiny yellow blossoms seemed to make both ponies frisky. You saw so much mustard around Spanish-speaking stock because they liked to nibble mustard about as much as humans did, concentrating instead on con-suming grass down to the root crowns.

Longarm intersected the main road near the river about three furlongs south of the ranch complex, and couldn't have said just why he reined in and turned in the saddle for a last look-see. But when he did he saw at least a dozen riders loping up that same entry lane under a cloud of dust. Their hats and darker outfits said they were Anglo from better than half a mile away. It was none of his own beeswax who they were or what they might want with old Consuela. A lady raising stock on a spread as big as this one—for he was still on her land—could be expected to have all sorts of visitors, and it wasn't as if she didn't have any grown men back yonder to protect her.

"Goddamn it, Creamy," he said to his mount. "I wasted a whole day getting Kinipai squared away, and Billy Vail never sent me all this way to fight with windmills like that asshole Don Quixote! I'm supposed to be down by that mysterious mesa right now. There's no mystery about Mexican land grants. Heaps of Anglo stockmen resent 'em, and it's a matter for the *local* law to deal with!"

Then he saw those distant riders reining in but not getting down in front of old Consuela's *casa*. Nobody seemed to be shooting at anyone yet. But Longarm sighed and said, "All right, just this once, but we really ought to watch this shit."

It took a bit less time loping back than it had taken to trot off. But as he closed in on the tense scene he saw the argument had had time to build up some steam. Consuela and half a dozen of her ranch hands were on her front veranda afoot. None of the riders had dismounted, and one scrawny old cuss was waving a paper at the Indian gal as if he wanted her to take it.

Everyone stopped jawing to stare at Longarm as he reined in to join the discussion. As he neared the man who seemed to be the process server and held out his free hand, Consuela cried, "Don't take that! You have to accept an eviction order before they can make it stick!"

Longarm smiled down at her reassuringly. "I fear you may know more about ranching than legal proceedings, Miss Consuela. That ain't the way things work, and even if it was, I don't own an acre of spit in these parts. So I'd best have a look-see."

He turned back to the mean-eyed old goat who'd been trying to serve the Indian gal with his fluttering single sheet, and mildly asked who he had the honor of confronting.

The older man said he was Cyrus Grayson of the Bar Three Slash, and asked who Longarm might be, aside from a Mex-lover.

Longarm ignored the snickers from the other riders backing the old goat's play as he mildly suggested, "By the time you found out exactly who I was, you might have decided you didn't want to know me all that well. What have you got there, Mister Grayson? Looks to me like a notarized letter."

Grayson handed it over, snapping, "Damned right it's notarized. Had it witnessed and sealed by a licensed notary public yesterday afternoon!"

Longarm scanned the absolutely worthless document with a smile of disbelief. Then he turned back to the worried Consuela and said, "This jasper knows no more about the law than you do, Miss Consuela. He's made a sworn statement to the effect that you are neither an American citizen nor a member of the white race, which is moot. Then he goes on to say you're squatting unlawfully on range he needs to get to the river road, and so on."

Grayson nodded grimly and added, "Signed, sealed, and delivered according to law. There's no arguing with papers witnessed and stamped by a notary public, right?"

Longarm laughed. "Wrong. A notary public is a respected tobacconist, innkeeper, or whatever, licensed by the county to witness and seal documents to prove he witnessed somebody swearing to him their words were true."

Grayson nodded. "That's what I just said."

Longarm replied, "No, it ain't. You tried to tell us this foolish scribble was a legal document. It's an expression of your personal opinion about a lady who was here first, on land you'd like to grab but ain't about to. I don't know what you paid to have this notarized, but you wasted your money.

Didn't the notary tell you when he stamped it for you that all he was backing was your word that you and you alone were the blithering idiot who signed it?"

Then Longarm was suddenly holding a pistol in his hand as the sheet of paper fluttered down between his mount's legs. So the younger rider on the far side of old Grayson suddenly let go of his own pistol grips with a sick grin as Longarm quietly said, "I only give one demonstration. The next one who reaches for his side arm had better mean it."

Old Grayson's face had gone frog-belly white, but his voice was fairly steady as he said, "Don't never do that again without my say-so, Rafe. Now get down and pick up that paper you made the man drop."

Longarm kept his gun out as he said, "I have a grander notion. I want Miss Consuela's lawyer to keep and cherish that free sample of documented stupidity."

He said a few words in Spanish. Consuela nodded, and one of her hands dashed forward as Longarm danced his mount off the paper.

Consuela asked something in Spanish. Longarm wanted both sides to get his message, so he replied in English. "It was a childish bluff I'd be ashamed to try in a lunatic asylum, Miss Consuela. I'd say your friendly neighbor's own lawyer told him there was no way they'd ever get a court order in New Mexico evicting anyone from an old Mexican land grant. So he wasted more time and money on a notarized document, as I said."

Grayson told the Mexican hand, "I'll take that," as the hand picked up the document in question. The Mexican hesitated. Longarm snapped at him in Spanish, and he ran clean past Consuela and into the house with it. Then Longarm told Grayson calmly, "You were trying to serve that paper on the lady, in front of witnesses. So now she's *got* it, and when her lawyers finish laughing at you, they'll likely want to hang on to it in case you ever try to waste their time in court again. Didn't your own lawyer explain any of this to you, old son?"

Grayson snapped, "I have my rights, damn it! I'm a U.S. citizen who fought at Cold Harbor for the Union and came away with scars to prove it. Who are you to take the side of a full-blood Indian against a good white American?"

Longarm chuckled fondly and replied, "I'll allow you seem to be a white American. I doubt you're all that *good,* and I know you're as smart as the average scarecrow. I don't know where you got the grand notion you could run a taxpaying grant-holder off her land as you might some Digger Indian poking through your trash heap, but it just ain't possible. So why don't you just git and save wear and tear on all concerned."

Grayson sat taller in his saddle as he grimly replied, "I don't run off as easy as your average Digger neither, Mex-lover."

Longarm said, "I don't think you understand this situation, land-grabber. It ain't going to work. Even if you shot everyone here and burned the whole spread to the ground, you would never in this world gain title to a Spanish grant recognized by the U.S. Government, unless you could get Miss Consuela here to marry up with you."

Neither Grayson nor the widow Llamas seemed enthusiastic about that suggestion. Longarm laughed and said, "You got to admit nothing *else* would work half so well. But seeing you haven't come courting, old son, why don't you just be on your way? If your pony has its feet stuck, I might be able to inspire it to run with a few pistol shots."

Grayson glared down at the comely widow on the veranda instead, snarling, "You win this hand, you stubborn squaw, but I can find me just as many hired guns as you, hear?"

Then he whirled his pony and rode off, his ragged-ass bunch in his wake, before Consuela could give the show away by saying anything at all.

As they rode off, cussing and arguing among themselves, Longarm holstered his six-gun, hauled out his Winchester, and dismounted to say, "I'd best stick around a while. I'm hoping you've seen the last of them till he comes up with another bright notion. But you never can tell what a wolverine might do when it can't seem to get a cupboard open."

She laughed girlishly, and suggested they have some more to eat and drink inside. He figured she had to do a lot of riding between snacks to keep her figure on the pleasant side of pleasantly plump. Her hired help, of course, took care of his riding stock and, as long as they were about it, relayed Longarm's suggestion that everyone get the kids, pigs, and chickens forted up inside the 'dobe walls for now.

Back in that same parlor, Longarm explained the situation in greater depth as they nibbled *tostadas* and sipped sangria punch made with plenty of rum. She asked if he didn't think a stupid enemy was more dangerous than a smart one. He didn't want to worry her more than he had to. So he shrugged and said, "Might be a smart move to send a message to your own law firm. Where are they—in Vado Seguro?"

She nodded, and said she'd send a rider right away. But he told her to hold the thought as he got out his notebook and a pencil stub, saying, "I saw a Western Union sign out front of the hardware store in town. I also have some pals over to Santa Fe, a lot closer to Governor Wallace than your lawyers might be, no offense. So we'd best alert the federal territorial government to this total idiot you're having trouble with."

She clapped her hands in delight, and asked if he could possibly stay until the troops came to bombard Cyrus Grayson into submission.

He chuckled and said, "Anything is possible, ma'am, but it ain't practical for me to man this post indefinitely. If nothing happens on this side of noon, I'll have to figure it's over, for now."

Then a rifle round spanged through the window to shatter the big pitcher on the table in front of the sofa and spatter them both with busted glass and sangria punch.

Sangria was made of red wine, lemonade, rum, and other crud that looked like bloody gashes on wet clothes and skin. But Longarm was out the door with his Winchester before he'd taken time to see whether either of them had been fatally wounded.

The rifleman was already well on his way aboard a roan, having fired blind from way off in the mustard, judging by the drifting white smoke. Longarm went back inside, muttering, "Looked like a kid. Might have been acting on his own. If there's one thing more dangerous than a blithering idiot, it has to be a *young* blithering idiot."

She'd risen to her feet, black lace sopping wet, and told him he was all spattered with sangria punch as he set down his Winchester again. He ruefully said he'd noticed as he regarded his own sleeves. His jeans hadn't caught too much of it, and he'd fortunately set his denim jacket aside, clear of the liquid explosion. But his hitherto light blue work shirt seemed covered with purple polka dots now.

As he picked up his notebook and pencil again, wiping the notebook's fake leather cover dry on his ruined shirt, he asked if she'd heard that table salt was good for fresh wine stains.

She said his only hope was a day-long soak in salt water, followed by thorough laundering and a day or so flapping in strong sunlight.

He grimaced and said, "I got another shirt in my saddlebags. I'd meant to launder some sweat out of it before I wore it some more. But it holds fond memories, and has to be an improvement over purple polka dots!"

As he sat down and proceeded to compose his wire to the federal men in Santa Fe, eighty-odd miles to the south-southeast, Consuela repeated what she'd said that morning about her late husband having been a big man. "I'm sure we can find you a pair of fresh shirts, and I would not feel as awkward handing down *your* freshly laundered work shirts to one of my larger riders, eh?"

He agreed that made sense. There was no need to go into why the personal duds of even a dead *hidalgo* might give some *vaqueros* lofty opinions of their position on the spread. He said he'd as soon wash up again before changing into that fresh shirt. When she said his wish was her command, he told her they'd best wait a spell. He'd already said that if the riders meant to come back, it would likely be before the day got hot enough for La Siesta.

But he felt sticky as hell long before noon as the sweet rum punch he'd been soaked with dried to the consistency of that goo on the shiny side of flypaper.

He scouted out around the buildings on foot, both to make sure he'd really run that last rider off and in hopes of feeling a tad less itchy. He couldn't find anyone to shoot. But he sure felt like shooting *somebody* as the morning dragged on.

Meanwhile, Consuela had bathed in her own quarters, and changed into a simple Mexican smock of white cotton, sashed at the waist with red silk. It made her look more girlish in her Junoesque Zuni way. That jasmine scent she'd splashed on her brown hide made her smell a lot more high-toned than your average lady in rope-soled sandals.

When she inquired, and he had to admit how miserable he still felt, she suggested he might bathe in her *mirador,* or what Anglo Victorians called a cupola when they had one stuck atop their own houses.

He allowed he'd noticed the boxlike structure atop her roof, but had assumed it to be a dovecote. She explained it had been built in wilder Apache times as a lookout and siege tower, with more to it than it might seem from outside, since the clay tiles of the sloped roof rose waist-high to anyone up there. She offered to show it to him, and must have taken it for granted that he'd cotton to it. For she called out to a house servant in passing that El Señor would be needing some hot bath water up there *poco tiempo.*

You had to go up a glorified ladder, or mighty steep staircase, by way of Consuela's own master bedchamber. It hadn't been meant to be easy for raiding Apache. Once they were up in the frame *mirador,* glazed with sash windows all around, Longarm saw it was fixed up as a sort of study or guest room, furnished with a writing table, a brass bedstead with blankets over the mattress, and the usual stools and such. She pointed out the big copper washtub under the table, and said she'd often bathed and slept naked during La Siesta in hot weather, when the cross ventilation that high off the ground was one's only hope.

He placed his Winchester on the writing table as he admired the view all around and said, "Raiders would have a time creeping in through the mustard with anyone watching from up here. For I'll be switched if I can't see lots of bare ground that would be behind the weeds to anyone sitting on the veranda downstairs!"

She said that was why her late husband's grandfather had built it that way to begin with. Then a small gal with a big *olla* of bathwater came up through the corner trap. So Longarm hauled the tub out, and she'd no sooner emptied her few gallons into it when yet another servant, this one a young boy, popped into view with even more warm water.

Folks back in Denver who'd started putting in newfangled indoor plumbing were already starting to forget how easy it was to get along without pipes when you could afford hot-and cold-running servants. They made it easier to bathe whenever or wherever you wanted, as well.

As the kids relayed his bathwater up from the kitchen, Consuela said she'd fetch him those shirts she'd mentioned. Her servants had already brought him plenty of Castile-style Spanish soap and a brace of Turkish towels.

By the time they had the copper tub half-filled, Longarm was sure nobody was creeping about out there in broad-ass daylight. So when he found himself alone, he stripped bare-ass to get right in the tub and wash away all that sticky sangria punch. It felt so good it gave him a hard-on. But he didn't think it showed above the soap suds when the lady of the house popped back up through the trap without letting him know she was coming.

She said she was sorry if she'd disturbed him, although she seemed more interested than embarrassed by the sight of his bare chest and wide shoulders. She held up one of the shirts she'd fetched and said she hoped it would suit him. He figured it was big enough. But it was a shade of dusky rose he'd have picked out for a lady's dress. The other shirt was spinach green, a more reasonable color for a man, but cut from silk satin, which looked even more sissy than the rosy poplin. He told her they both looked swell, since either was an improvement on soiled or wine-stained work shirts and he didn't want to insult her by implying her Carlos had been a foppish dresser. He knew she was fixing to brag on handing the duds down to a famous lawman who'd admired them. He also knew he was admired in some Mexican circles, and disliked in others, because he couldn't stand El Presidente Dias and his brutal *rurales*.

When he said he liked both shirts, she scooped up his stained one to run it down to the kitchen. He finished washing, rose to his feet in the tub, and began to rinse his naked body off with an extra pot of clean water. So Consuela caught him standing there, bare-ass with a hard-on, when she popped back up to ask something else. She stared goggled-eyed for as long as it took her to blush beet red under her tan, and then dropped out of sight again as he began to blush a bit himself.

The next time she wanted to come up through the trap she knocked on a stair tread and called out to him. He said he was decent, and she looked in and found him seated on a stool near a window with just a towel wrapped around the parts that mattered. He said, "You were right about cross ventilation and how warm this valley can get by noon. I figured it was all right for me to keep watch informally, seeing you've already learned all my secrets in any case."

She flustered that he was a naughty boy as she came all the way up with a tray of fresh *tostadas* and rum punch, made this time with just the lemon, sugar, and *yerba buena,* a sort of dry-country mint Spanish-speaking folks fancied more than some.

She set the refreshments on the wide windowsill, and closed the trapdoor as she allowed it did seem about time for La Siesta. Longarm didn't ask why she'd chosen to flop down on the bedstead instead of down below in her more private quarters. He was no fool, and even if he had been, she was sending mighty warm smoke signals with those smoldering sloe eyes. So he poured them two tumblers of punch and sat down on the blankets beside her, saying, "I doubt anyone's out for another fuss under the noonday sun."

Then he tasted his drink and declared, "You sure were generous with the white rum this time, Miss Consuela."

She demurely replied, "I thought it would save having to go back down for more. Are you aware that towel is giving away your secrets again?"

It didn't seem to bother her. But he glanced down to see that, just as he'd thought, he was covered tolerably well. He said, "I suspect that's just a big wrinkle in this Turkish toweling, ma'am."

She made a thoughtful grab for it as she murmured, "So you say."

He laughed and said he knew how to play *bego-bego* as well as any Na-déné gal as he grabbed her by one big soft cantaloupe and they both flopped back across the bedding. She laughed back and said she wasn't any fool Apache as she made a more skillful grab for him and gasped, "Madre de Dios, you *are* a big man, aren't you!"

He kissed her and ran his free hand down her considerable curves to see what *she* had down yonder. Anyone who said all Indian gals were much the same had likely never felt up all that many Indian gals—or white gals for that matter. Longarm was used to finding every gal's crotch far different from every other, bless each and every one of them. But even as he commenced to strum her old banjo with skilled wet fingers, he felt obliged to warn her, "I did say I'd be riding on this side of forever, didn't I, *querida?*"

She began to move her bigger hips in a way far different from the smaller and younger Kinipai as she moaned, "Faster. Did you think I would have been in this much of a hurry if I had thought you were liable to stay longer? A woman has needs, but a woman trying for to maintain her dignity with her servants must give some thought to whom she wishes for to *chingar*, eh?"

So he kissed her again and got rid of the toweling, shoved her thin skirting up around her soft brown waist and rolled his hips between her big brown welcoming thighs to conjugate naughty Spanish verbs in her. Consuela gasped in surprised delight, and laughed like hell as he thrust in and out of her muttering, *"Chingar, chingo, chinge, chingamos,* and what else?"

She commenced to peel the rest of her white cotton off over her head as she sobbed, *"La vida es breve. Vamonos pa'l carajo y vamos a joder toda la fregeda tarde!"*

He said that sounded fair. He figured he was stuck there for at least the whole damned afternoon, and there were far more tedious ways to pass the time than strong drink and hot fornication. So once he had her spread out under him as naked as an enthusiastic jay, he hooked his elbows under her plump knees to position her even better.

She stared up at him in mingled fear and adoration and said she'd never taken it at that angle so deep before. But when he asked if she wanted him to back off, she dug her nails into his bare bouncing buttocks and hissed, *"Lo que necesito! Pero me marvillo que todavia estoy vivo!"*

So he agreed he needed it just as bad, and found it just as amazing that they seemed to be living through it when he shot his wad and kept on pounding as he felt her warm wet innards responding in kind. So by the time he'd brought her to climax he was hot as hell again, and things went on that way for a delightfully long time before they had to stop for a breather.

They enjoyed more rum punch and tobacco while they were at it. He stood tall to light up and check the sunlit horizon all around as Consuela refilled their tumblers, wondering aloud if she'd brought enough liquid refreshments for a wilder siesta than she'd planned. She didn't deny it when Longarm accused her of planning something when she'd slipped into that easy-to-slip-out-of outfit. She held out his tumbler to him, and demurely confessed she'd been curious to learn if half the things they said about El Brazo Largo could be true. When he sat down beside her to share the cheroot as well, she giggled and said she'd been expecting less.

She asked if she could count on him staying at least a week or so. He lay back across the bed and hauled her down to nestle her head on his bare chest as he set the tumbler of rum punch aside and replied, "I'd be proud to spend at least a month with anyone half as friendly, you pretty thing. But to tell the truth, my boss, Marshal Billy Vail, would have a fit if he knew I was off saving damsels in distress from dragons. So let's study on that dragon called Grayson, starting with why he's so anxious to extend his own range as far as El Rio Chama."

She began to run the cool bottom of her drink up and down his bare belly as she absently mused, "There are other cattle trails off to the east. Perhaps he just wants more water for his stock, no?"

Longarm said, "No. There's well-watered mountains to either side of this valley with heaps of cleaner seeps and springs than the muddy main stream. You know I met some of your *vaqueros* stringing a drift fence on the far side of the Chama up the slope a ways. So might the original Llamas grant extend as far as the Jicarilla line?"

She said, "*Pero* no. Only out to the Camino del Rey, or what you now call the coach road. But you must have seen my holdings are not fenced, and your own Anglo law allows stray stock for to graze on any federal land not set aside for anything else by the government, eh?"

He nodded and dryly observed, "I'm sure lots of your cows wind up wading such a modest river all by themselves. Keeping them off that Indian land with drift wire makes sense too. Old Cyrus Grayson must have noticed the grass looks greener on the far side of the fence. I suspect he's after easier access to that ungrazed reservation range."

She protested, "Is reserved for Los Apaches, no?"

He nodded soberly, but said, "The powers that be are fixing to move the Jicarilla south and free up all that ungrazed grass and uncut timber. Anglo stockmen such as Grayson are in closer touch with the powers that be."

He set his smoke aside and took her glass from his belly to sip some rum punch before he handed it back. "I wish I knew exactly which powers were behind such an ill-timed move. I just helped the War Department calm some other Indians down, over to the Four Corners. So I know General Sherman ain't anxious to needlessly upset peaceful Apache types whilst three or more regiments are playing tag with Victorio, for Pete's sake!"

She sounded sort of prim as she observed her own Indian kin had long since learned to get along better with Mexican and Anglo neighbors who were just as tough but far easier-going than Apache. He got the distinct impression nobody else in northern New Mexico, Anglo, Mexican, Zuni, or Tanoan, would shed one tear for poor little Kinipai and her Jicarilla kin when—not if—they were evicted from their big fat reservation.

He said, "You should have seen the stampede when the Lakota were forced out of the Black Hills. Prospectors and land-grabbers came from all over, along with the male and female parasites and human birds of prey such booms attract. The Dulce Agency could wind up as wild as Deadwood by the time we got things under control again."

He knew he hadn't planned on confiding more than he had to. But he figured she was apt to gossip when he'd gone on in any case. In the meantime, there was no saying what other gossip a local gal might have heard. So he confided, "I've been trying to learn more about a whole heap of armed and mysterious strangers moving into these parts, honey. They seem to be Anglo and may be hired guns."

She polished off the last of her rum punch and got rid of the dry tumbler as she casually replied, "We've heard such talk, *querido*. I think that may be why Cyrus Grayson accused you of being just such a rider. He could see you were not one of my regular *vaqueros,* and there has been much gossip about Regulators up by this end of the territory."

Longarm whistled softly and said he hoped it was just gossip. For the Lincoln County War to the south was officially over, and that noisy confusion had commenced when one faction bought control of the elected sheriff and another, led by merchants and stockmen with less political pull, had "deputized" their own force of ad hoc "Regulators" under the *posse comitatus* provisions of common law.

It hadn't worked, of course. The corrupt lawmen recognized by the Santa Fe Ring had refused to recognize the private-agency badges worn by McSween riders such as

Billy the Kid, and so a rooting, tooting, and shooting time had been had by all before Governor Wallace had come west to declare such shit must cease. But the notion that private citizens could recruit and arm their own Regulator forces to enforce the law as it seemed it ought to be enforced had never faded all the way away.

He decided, "Old Cyrus wouldn't have taken me for a hired gun from other parts if he knew that much about hired guns from other parts. So I suspect you're only up against a proddy pest your ownself."

She asked if he'd forgotten that rifle ball through the window down below. He reminded her he'd already said that had likely been an eager whelp. "By now he's been whupped with a newspaper and warned to behave. For kids don't act so foolish unless they expect to brag and be praised for their heroism. Old Cyrus is a fool, but not that big a fool. He was trying to bluff a dumb Mexican neighbor, no offense. He'd have never come up with that pathetic bluff if he'd known where to get his hands on a so-called Regulator."

Consuela rose on one elbow and groped across him for the other half-filled tumbler. It felt swell. She had great tits. She drained the tumbler, then rolled clean over him—that felt even better—to perch on the edge of the mattress and pour them both fresh drinks as she pleaded with him to at least guard her from that cruel gringo neighbor until sundown.

It would have been as cruel to say he meant to be on his way by that time. So he suggested she get on her hands and knees so he could make sure nobody was creeping up on them outside at the moment.

She was willing, and he really could see all around below as he got a good grip on her heroic hips to take her from behind, tall in his socks. By this time they'd gotten to where it just felt swell instead of desperately thrilling. So he got to wondering, as he stood there calmly banging away, how many other gents had stood watch up here the same way over so many years of off-and-on Indian troubles. He doubted he was the first who'd discovered standing guard all by oneself could get tedious as hell. It was surprising how easy it was to just stand and stare with one's old organ-grinder up inside a pal.

Chapter 9

He rode off in that tricky light near sundown when any rider a snoop might spot at a distance would be tough to describe. He'd put on that green satin shirt and started out aboard the palomino, leading the cream this time. Not wanting to ride back to the trail town of Vado Seguro, he'd asked anyone answering those wires sent from there to reply care of Western Union at Loma Blanca, to the south and hence closer to where Billy Vail had ordered him to go in the first damned place.

There were others on the road that early in the evening, although they were widely spaced as he howdied those he met going the other way. He set a fair pace for anyone going the same way to overtake. So nobody seemed to. He rode at a trot for an hour, and let both ponies water in the shallows of the Chama and browse some cottonwood leaves as he changed mounts by moving the shaken-out saddle blanket, and then, of course, the saddle, back aboard the cream mare. He took his time to rest them more than to water and browse them. They'd been watered and fed cracked corn before leaving El Rancho Llamas. But it seldom hurt to give a horse more water, and they couldn't bloat their fool selves on leathery cottonwood leaves. Swamp maple was about the only really dangerous browse a pony would willingly eat too much of, and you hardly ever saw swamp maple in these parts.

He remounted and rode on, making even better time because, just as he'd remembered, that mare was the high-stepper of the pair. The sexless palomino came along willingly, packing nothing, at the quicker pace.

He'd swapped mounts again, more than once, by the time he rode into the sounds of a distant piano and spied pinpoints of light down the road ahead. Loma Blanca, despite its old Spanish handle, had a more Anglo feel to it as Longarm reined in near the black-and-yellow Western Union sign across from a busy-looking saloon.

He tethered his ponies to the hitch rail, and strode in to see if anyone had seen fit to answer any of his earlier wires sent from Vado Seguro by way of that Llamas rider.

There was one answer, from a territorial lawman Longarm knew in Santa Fe. They'd heard of Cyrus Grayson. They had him down, rightly or wrongly, as one of those pests called "litigious" by lawyers and judges because they enjoyed litigation, or bringing others to law, as much as a hog loved his wallow on a hot day in August. Santa Fe said they'd look into Grayson's possible abuse of due process, although there wasn't much of a mystery as to how you persuaded a cigar-stand notary to witness and stamp your fool signature on most anything. Grayson wasn't known to have ever pushed one of his many petty feuds to gunplay, however.

Longarm hadn't told anyone south of Denver what he might be doing down this way, so the lawman hadn't expressed any opinion about the peculiar activity around La Mesa de los Viejos, or the plans of either the BIA or the Indians in regard to that big Jicarilla drive.

Billy Vail never wasted five cents a word answering progress reports unless he had further orders to give a deputy in the field, of course.

Longarm went back out front and, staying afoot as men just love to do after hours in the saddle, he led his ponies down to the livery they'd told him about at the Western Union, and asked the Mexican night crew if they'd rub down and rest, but just water his riding stock so he could ride on before midnight.

When they said they could, he took his saddle gun and some lighter valuables worth stealing with him to that saloon. He'd eaten plenty of tortillas and beans at Consuela's for supper and it was still early. But a man sure felt like another beer after pissing along the trail a spell, and you never knew what gossip you'd hear in a trail-town saloon.

He got some thoughtful looks but no unfriendly stares when he passed through the swinging doors to see who might be playing the piano so poorly. The crowd seemed mostly Anglo, with just a few Mexicans playing dominos at a corner table. He saw to his chagrin that the piano was being badly played by a skinny old gent in a striped shirt and brocaded vest. He'd thought for a moment it might be Miss Red Robin, an old pal who played the poorest rendition of "Aura Lee" and gave the best French lessons west of the Mississippi.

But why on earth would a man want to dwell on such country matters after spending all that recent time in a cunt?

He decided it was all the dark-complected company he'd been keeping of late. The two Indian gals had been of different anatomy as well as tribal background, but the henna-rinsed Red Robin was one of those naturally blue-eyed brunettes with skin as creamy as that high-stepping mare down the way. He ordered a needled beer from the politely stone-faced barkeep, and had to grin as he consoled himself with the simple fact he'd never been as loco with his old organ-grinder as some he'd heard about.

When an old drunk standing next to him asked what was so funny, Longarm knew the poor old-timer didn't really care. But he signaled the barkeep to refill the drunk's beer schooner anyway as he smiled and explained, "Just thinking about horny riders and the dumb things they can do when they're hard up."

As the barkeep drew another for him the old-timer said, "Horny riders are always hard up. That's why I feel safer around *drinking* men. But get to the funny part, old son."

Longarm said, "There was this Prussian cavalry officer I read about, back in the time of old Freddy the Great. Seems he fell in love with this young mare in heat, likely a buckskin, whose rump reminded him of some fat gal back home. So they caught him standing up behind her on a box, humping away with his fancy pants down."

The barkeep put the second beer before them as he said with a puzzled smile, "They caught a man humping a horse? A full-grown one?"

Longarm sipped some of his own suds and explained. "A mare in heat, with a tendency to pucker down hard. But them Prussian officers felt it was a mighty odd way for a man to behave too. So they court-martialed him for conduct unbecoming a human being, and they were fixing to shoot him when old Freddy the Great got word of it."

The drunk asked, "You mean King Freddy forgave the cuss for acting so forward with a cavalry mount?"

Longarm shook his head and said, "Not hardly. Freddy the Great agreed the poor simp didn't belong in the cavalry. So he ordered him transferred to the infantry, and that way, everybody came out all right. I reckon they found a proper stud for the mare, and I understand the Prussian army provides drummer boys for old infantry hands who've been away from home a spell."

The three of them laughed.

102

A morose-looking young squirt a couple of paces down the bar said, "I don't think that's funny, Julesburg," in a mighty unfriendly tone.

The drunk between them crawfished away from the bar with his free drink as Longarm smiled thoughtfully down the mahogany and asked if anyone was speaking to him under the impression his handle might be Julesburg.

The kid, sporting knee-length chinked chaps and an ivory-gripped Merwin Hulbert over sun-faded denim, sounded sure of himself as he replied, "We figured out who you had to be, Julesburg. A tall rider with his hat telescoped Colorado-style and his Colt worn cross-draw adds up to one such cuss with the sand to stand up to a dozen white men for the money and other favors of a Mex gal. We both know I have the dishonor to be addressing the one and only Julesburg Kid, a mite older but no wiser than when he rode with Black Jack Slade up Julesburg way, seeing his manners still seem to reckless."

Longarm blinked, then had to laugh as he figured out who the kid had to be. He said, "There *was* a young cowboy wearing chinked chaps in that bunch with old Cyrus Grayson. After that you've got things a tad mixed up, old son."

The barkeep backed away and the place got mighty quiet when the kid almost sobbed, "I ain't your son. My mama was married up when I was born. I'm Jason Townsend, and I got my own rep as a man nobody had best mess with, hear?"

Longarm nodded soberly and said, "In that case I'd rather buy you a beer than mess with you, Jason."

The kid said, "I don't drink with back-shooting sons of bitches."

The barkeep half moaned, "Jesus H. Christ!" One of the Mexican domino players murmured, *"Vamanos, amigos. Tengo que mear como el demonio!"*

So all the customers decided they had to piss like the devil, whether they spoke Spanish or not. The barkeep just lit out the back way without saying anything.

Longarm said quietly, "I can overlook that part about my probable parentage, seeing we seem to have the place to ourselves, if you'd be kind enough to tell me just who this Julesburg Kid ever shot in the back. I ain't him. But since I seem to remind you of some hired gun with a nasty rep . . ."

Then he read the sidestep away from the bar for what it meant and snapped, "Don't try it, Jason. I know Merwin Hulbert still makes those cheap shiny thumb-busters, but it was never a good fighting gun to begin with and I don't want to prove that to you, boy!"

Young Townsend snarled, "I'll show you who's a boy! I'd heard you'd lost your nerve. Heard that was how come you back-shot that brand inspector with no rep of his own. You ain't got the grit to slap leather face-to-face with another gunfighter, eh?"

Longarm muttered, "Aw, shit, you're supposed to be a gunfighter as well as a total asshole?"

It was the wrong thing to say to a punk on the prod. Townsend had been working himself up all the time he'd been trailing his intended victim. So he moved fast, faster than most, as his gun hand swooped down on those side-draw ivory grips.

Then he was reeling along the bar with his cheap fancy gun still in its holster and two hundred grains of hot lead cooling off inside his ruptured but still-convulsing heart. As Longarm followed his last movements with a smoking but now-silent Winchester, the boy bawled out, "Don't whup me no more and I'll be good, Mama!"

Then he landed facedown in the sawdust with one spur still ringing like a coin spinning down as Longarm muttered, "I told you not to try, you poor dumb kid!"

As the smoke cleared, the barkeep came back in with a somewhat older gent wearing a silvery mustache and matching pewter badge. So Longarm started to identify himself as he finished reloading.

Before he could do so, the town marshal firmly stated, "I don't want to hear your sad story. Kevin here just told me the punk-ass was the one who started it, and no jury would ever hang a man who'd been called a son of a bitch to his face in public."

Longarm put his gun away and just paid attention to his elders as the town law continued. "I'd hold you for the coroner's hearing anyways, if I liked noise. But rightly or wrongly, you just now gunned the black-sheep son of a mighty big and mighty close cattle clan I'd as soon not mess with in an election year. So why don't you do us both a favor and ride on, Julesburg?"

Longarm managed not to grin as he quietly replied, "I see great minds do run in the same channels. I'd only stopped here to wet my whistle on my way to—"

"Don't tell us where you're headed and we won't have to tell the Townsends," the town law said. "Nobody with a lick of sense is about to lie to the Townsends about anything involving the spilled blood of even a *worthless* Townsend. And I don't want to have to tidy up after any local voters neither. So how come you're just standing there like a big-ass bird, stranger?"

Longarm allowed he was just leaving and left, crabbing to one side as he stepped out the swinging doors into the darkness. But nobody gathered outside seemed more than curious as he bulled his way through and crossed over to the livery.

One of the Mexican hostlers said he'd figured El Brazo Largo would want one of his *caballos* saddled in a hurry, and so he'd taken the liberty of cinching that stock saddle to the fresher-looking mare.

Longarm nodded soberly, but said, "Seeing you've guessed who I might be, I shouldn't have to tell you why I'd rather

105

ride on aboard less distinctive horseflesh. What sort of a swap might you be willing to make for danged near pure Spanish barbs?"

The hostler grinned like a kid smelling fresh-baked pie while coming home from school, and said, "Take your pick from our remuda out in the corral. In God's truth we don't have stock to match either of those two you rode in with. *Pero* we may be able to send you on your way with reliable if less distinguished riding stock, eh?"

They could. Longarm rode out of town before midnight aboard one bay and leading another. In the meantime he'd changed shirts. Everyone who'd been there would recall a stranger in a green satin shirt as the intended victim of the late Jason Townsend. The one thing anyone could say for dusky-rose poplin was that it didn't look at all like green satin.

Chapter 10

Longarm wouldn't have entered either fresh mount in a serious horse race, but he found them both steady and willing. So along about two in the morning he tried crossing back over the river to the less traveled side.

He suspected he'd picked the wrong ford when the river came up to his knees and filled his boots. But as long as he was at it, he took off his telescoped Stetson and bent down with it to fill the crown with more water.

Once the felt had taken the time to soften some, he punched the crown all the way plain, and then creased it along the top and dimpled both sides cavalry-style.

He didn't meet up with any Apache war parties on their side of the river as he worked his way south through timber and chaparral. The reservation line doglegged far off to the west this far south, and he suspected the Jicarilla were more worried about *pindah lickoyee* than vice versa about now.

Well before dawn he recrossed the Chama to get back on that coach road and follow it north. He didn't want to go back to see Consuela. despite fond memories of her rollicking tawny rump. He knew the trail town of Camino Viejo stood by the river just to the southwest of La Mesa de los Viejos.

You just about had to pass close by to get to the old Indian pathway up to those canyonlands, and all in all, he figured it might be best if folks recalled him coming from the south instead of the scene of that dumb gunplay to the north.

As the sunrise caught him still in the saddle, Longarm peeled off his denim jacket and put that away with the green shirt to ride into town outstandingly rosy from the gunbelt up.

He wasn't too surprised to see that despite its Spanish name the trail town, handy to more than one trail, was far more Anglo than Mexican. There was always Mexican or Indian hired help in any New Mexican town for the same reasons the shoeshine boys and street sweepers tended to be colored east of Austin. But neither Mexicans nor Indians with money to pick and choose seemed to cotton to Camino Viejo, situated as it was between an Apache reserve and a heap of haunted ghost towns.

He left the two bays in an Anglo-run livery near the Western Union. He didn't have anything new to wire anyone, and he hadn't told anyone to wire him here in Camino Viejo. So he idly traced the single line of telegraph wire east against the morning sky for as far as he could tell, then took himself and his Winchester to breakfast at the hotel dining room recommended by the livery hands.

There were always a few late risers having breakfast at seven in the morning. So Longarm knew the blandly pretty waitress answered to Trisha before she came over to take his order. He'd already read the blackboard on the wall, the place not being prissy enough to hand out printed literature, and said, "Them waffles with scrambled eggs and sausages sound tempting, Miss Trisha. But could I have mine with chili con carne instead of syrup over 'em?"

The slender dishwater blonde told him it was his funeral. Then, just as she was fixing to take his order to the kitchen, she turned back to him with a puzzled smile and asked, "Do I know you, Mister . . . ?"

"My friends call me Henry," Longarm lied, figuring drunk or sober he'd be able to recall the clerk who played the type-writer for Billy Vail. He didn't push his luck by insisting he'd met Trisha before. But she suddenly smiled—it was a great improvement in her looks—and said, "Oh, sure, I remember that dark cavalry hat and mustache now. You told us you'd fought those rebs at Apache Canyon during the war, last time you passed through with that big market drive."

He neither confirmed nor denied her accusation. He liked to ask trick questions too. So she lit out for the kitchen to fetch him his substantial if unusual breakfast.

He was enjoying it, his Winchester across his lap, when a couple of new customers came in, dressed cow and covered with dust. They gave Longarm a long look and took a cor-ner table. When Trisha came out to ask what they wanted, Longarm politely waited until she'd taken their order before he called out, "Hold on, Miss Trisha. The next time you get a chance could I have me some cream for this coffee?"

She nodded easily and said, "Sure you can. But I thought you said before you cottoned to it black, Henry."

The strange riders exchanged glances as Longarm smiled sheepishly and said, "You've made it stronger than usual this morning, no offense."

The waitress didn't seem to care one way or the other. A short spell later she'd fetched him a can of condensed milk and served the two others their white bread and beans with black coffee. Longarm was glad the coffee really was brewed strong, the way he liked it.

The other two would have doubtless finished their lighter breakfasts ahead of him in any case. But Longarm gave them plenty of time by ordering a slab of cheesecake and more coffee to go with his after-breakfast smoke. So they and some of the other customers had left, and Longarm was about to, when he heard the waitress hissing like she'd cut herself, and turned to see a burly young cuss in bib overalls had her by one wrist and didn't seem to want to let go as he grinned up at her like a shit-eating hound.

Longarm knew better. He'd just ridden out of one dumb scrape with an aspiring desperado, and gals who didn't want assholes falling in love with them had no business waiting tables. But when Trisha sobbed, "Damn it, Alvin, you're hurting me!" Longarm just naturally found himself saying, "Stop hurting her, Alvin."

The burly lout let go of the gal's skinny wrist, but rose to his own considerable height as he scowled Longarm's way and demanded, "Were you talking to me, cowboy?"

The question hardly deserved an answer, but Longarm had just found out how dumb it could be to call a scowling asshole an asshole. So he kept his own voice mild as he replied, "Somebody had to. Trisha, why don't you go rustle up more coffee for me and Alvin whilst we have us a word in private?"

The pallid blonde pleaded, "Please don't have a fight in here, boys. It could mean my job!"

Then Longarm got to his own feet and, seeing how tall he rose, Trisha sobbed, "Oh, Dear Lord!" and tore out of the room.

Alvin was looking itchy-footed too as he stared down at the saddle gun in Longarm's big fist and the .44-40 on his hip, saying, "Hold on, Mister Henry. I ain't armed and it ain't as if I really hurt your gal, right?"

Longarm moved over to the heavier man's table, scaring the shit out of old Alvin but smiling pleasantly enough as he explained, "I knew all the time you were only funning, Alvin. But you're a man of the world. So you can surely see the fix the two of us poor innocent gents are in. You know how gals expect a man to stick up for them when they let out a holler. You know *you'd* have had to call *me*, no matter how you really felt, had I been teasing your *own* gal, right?"

Alvin suddenly grinned boyishly and said, "Say no more, Hank. I didn't know the gal was spoken for and if it's all the same with you, I'd rather just drop the matter than fight over a gal who'd only call me a big bully if I won!"

Longarm laughed and asked, "Lord have mercy, has that happened to you too?"

So they were shaking on it when Trisha and the cook risked a peek through the kitchen doors. But she never came out till her burly admirer had left, leaving a handsome dime on the table instead of the usual nickel. Then she asked, her blue eyes staring astounded, "How did you *do* that, Henry? The last time anyone told Alvin to leave me alone there was broken chinaware and busted-up furniture all over the place!"

Longarm said, "I told him a white lie about us. Is it safe to say you don't have any other gent here in town to stick up for you?"

She sighed. "The few who might have shown any interest all seem afraid of Alvin. He's the town blacksmith and they say he can bend horseshoes with his bare hands. What you did was awfully sweet, Henry. But if I were you I'd ride. I can handle Alvin without resorting to gunplay. But you may wind up with a harder row to hoe!"

Longarm finished his coffee—she hadn't brought any more—and left the right change on his own table without sitting down as he said, "I doubt we'll have a duel over you, no offense. I mean to ride on. But I've had a long night in the saddle and daytime ain't the best time to travel here and now. So I reckon I'll hire a hotel bed upstairs and stay out of sight and study war no more till suppertime."

She told him he was cutting it thin, then spotted the quarter tip he was leaving and allowed she hoped to serve him some more at suppertime.

He ambled through the archway into the hotel lobby next door. An old jasper who looked as hearty as one of their dusty paper fern plants or the dusty elk's head over the key

111

counter, stared hard at the Winchester Longarm had toted in by way of baggage and said he could have a corner room for six bits, payment in advance.

He brightened some when Longarm paid with a silver cartwheel and allowed he'd take the change in the form of not being disturbed one moment before he damned well decided to wake up and come back down for his supper.

The corner room offered cross ventilation and a view of the river, meaning it would be on the sunny side after high noon. But when Longarm shut the jalousies he saw there was far more breeze than light coming up through the slanted slats.

He bolted the hall door, stripped to the buff, and flopped naked atop the turned-down bedding to discover that, once he was able to take a load off his feet and clear his mind of listening for distant hoofbeats in the dark, he was more tuckered than he'd expected.

He was sound asleep in no time, unaware of the conversation those two advance scouts were having about him in the saloon across from his hotel.

The mean-looking Granddaddy Townsend was holding court at a corner table as the younger and faster-riding kinsmen of the late Jason Townsend remained standing, as if they were schoolboys reporting to their teacher to explain piss-poor grades. One insisted, "We've scouted high and we've scouted low, Granther. The only stranger to anyone we talked to here in Camino Viejo won't work as the bastard who shot it out with our Jason."

The grim, grizzled Granddaddy Townsend snapped, "Nobody shot it out with the dumb kid. Jason drew on a known gunfighter who was standing there with his damned carbine in his damned hand!"

The bitter old man looked away as he muttered, "Jason was a fool kid and I always knew he was going to die young and dumb, but blood calls to blood. You say there's only *one* such stranger?"

One of the Townsend riders who'd been in the hotel dining room with Longarm said, "Tall, tanned cuss with a mustache, somewhere in his late twenties or early thirties, just as they described that son of a bitch who gunned Jason. But after that he seemed to be known here."

The old man snapped, "He had to be known *some* damned where, and we know he wasn't from Loma Blanca, damn his eyes!"

The younger Townsend, who'd heard Trisha call Longarm Henry, said, "After that, he wore his hat crushed cavalry instead of Colorado. Had on a sissy pink shirt instead of the green one they told us about up in Loma Blanca. Everyone with any sense favors a six-gun and Winchester loading the same .44-40 brass in Apache Country. But he's over to the Hotel de Paris if you want us to fetch him for you, Granther."

The old man might have told them to. Then two more of his boys came in, blinking like owls as their eyes adjusted to the change from the dazzling sunlight out front. One called out, "We found some riding stock that don't belong to nobody here in town, Granther. Stranger left 'em at the town livery. Said he meant to bed down a spell and ride on in the cool of evening."

The mean old man growled, "Never mind what he might be doing here. Which way was he coming from and what was he riding?"

The second of the two who'd found those bays at the nearby livery said, "Seems he rid in from the south on one bay gelding, leading a second. One's a redder shade of chestnut than the other and they both have white blazes but different brands. Don't know what you'd call either, seeing the Mex brands look more like kids' scribbles than the letters and numbers real *rancheros* register."

Granddaddy Townsend made a prune face and said, "Never mind all that. Any rider on the dodge can circle a town to come in from any direction. But that Julesburg Kid who murdered our Jason rode into Loma Blanca earlier astride a white barb and leading a palomino, in a green shirt, not no pink one. You say this jasper you other boys saw eating breakfast at the hotel knew somebody there?"

One of them nodded and said, "The waitress called him Henry. They acted sweet on one another, like he'd come courting."

The old man rose from his seat, patting the worn grips of his Walker Conversion as he decided, "We're wasting time. No killer on the owlhoot trail slows down to court waitress gals this close to the scene of his crime! Having no known business in these parts, that Julesburg Kid is doubtless on his way to that stagecoach line to Fort Wingate and points West, unless he's streaking for Old Mexico in hopes of escaping us entire. So *vamanos, muchachos.* I want the head of that murderous drifter, and he sure as hell don't seem to be here in Camino Viejo!"

As the bunch of them strode out of the saloon, boot heels thudding and spurs jingling, the barkeep who'd been listening silently turned to signal what looked like a regular customer sipping suds down the bar.

That wasn't exactly what the man was there for. The barkeep asked if he'd been following all that war talk. The hired gun nodded casually and said, "I'm paid to notice trouble. Didn't sound like trouble for anyone *we* know, though."

The barkeep said, "Boss lady says she likes to hear everybody's troubles hereabouts. You'd best go tell her what just blew into town."

The hired gun protested, "Shit, that federal deputy they want us to watch out for wears a dark brown outfit, not no pink shirt."

The barkeep said, "Tell her anyways. They say Longarm's been known to act sort of sneaky."

Chapter 11

Longarm arose around five that afternoon feeling way better. He flung open the jalousies so he could see what he was doing as he gave himself a whore-bath and shaved at the corner washstand. He had to put on the same rosy shirt, but it smelled all right. Then he went down to see what they might be serving for supper, having slept clean by his usual noon dinner.

He found there was nobody else having supper at that hour, if anyone living in town ate supper out to begin with. When he commented on this to the same waitress, the dishwater blonde said they had to stay open lest travelers stopping at the hotel go hungry. But there didn't seem to be all that many since all that talk about Apache trouble had started up again.

Longarm was tempted to assure her the Jicarilla seemed resigned to their unfair fate. But he never did. What Billy Vail had sent him to look into was no beeswax of anyone else. So he allowed that roast beef with mashed potatoes and string beans sounded fine, if they'd leave out the string beans and serve him some of the tamales mentioned on the blackboard instead. When she said they could, but it would cost him extra, he said to deal him that hand anyway.

So they did, and he was right about hot tamales tasting far more interesting than string beans. A couple of townsmen in frock coats came in, but only had coffee, and left as Longarm was ordering dessert. He noticed that as Trisha was clearing away his dinner dishes, she was singing soft and low that old Scotch song about rye whiskey. He'd have never followed her words if he hadn't already known them. But seeing he did, he had to grin as their possible double meaning sank in. She'd said that she didn't have anybody here in Camino Viejo, but she still seemed to be singing:

> "Among the train, there is a swain
> I dearly love mysel'.
> But what's his name and where's his hame,
> I dinna choose to tell!"

It was a shame he had all that riding ahead of him around the time she'd be getting off, but that was the way things went some nights. So he had apple pie with cheddar cheese, put away another strong cup of coffee, and told her he might or might not see her again at breakfast time.

She really seemed to care as she asked whether he'd be staying on at the hotel or not. So he said, "We live in an uncertain world, Miss Trisha. I got some calls to make this evening. Ain't sure how many or how long."

She asked, "Are you some sort of cattle buyer or traveling salesman, Henry? They were wondering about that this afternoon."

He said, "You might say I'm interested in horse-trading. Who did you say wanted to know?"

She shrugged. "Queen Kirby, I imagine. It was some of her help, not Queen Kirby herself, of course. You saw two more of them just now. Having coffee at that table near the door?"

Longarm nodded and said, "Figured they were looking me over. I take it this Queen Kirby is the biggest frog in this little puddle, no offense?"

Trisha made a wry face and replied, "None taken. I don't think much of Camino Viejo, either, but a girl needs a job. Queen Kirby's all right, I reckon. She owns most everything and everybody in town, but she's never done me dirty and I was brung up to live and let live."

Longarm said, "I thought you sounded like a decent country gal. I take it this Queen Kirby don't own this dining room, though?"

Trisha said, "Nor the hotel, the two churches, or mayhaps a few of the shops down the street. Once you own the saloon, the card house, the, ah, houses of ill repute, and the municipal corral, you've got a pretty firm hold on things, though."

He nodded. "I follow your drift. There seems to be some such big frog in every puddle this size. Not too many of 'em seem to be gals called queens, though. Is that her first name or an honorary title, Miss Trisha?"

The blonde said she didn't know, explaining, "I've only seen her out front in passing. She never eats here. I understand she has a Chinee cook and dines on frog legs, fish eggs, and peasant-birds at her fancy mansion just outside of town."

Longarm smiled gently and said, "I think *pheasant* was the bird you had in mind. But you were right about such vittles sounding a mite fancy. I've known rich folks who ate natural as the rest of us. So it's likely this Queen Kirby ain't been rich as long. I reckon I could use another coffee, ma'am. Seeing others seem so interested in me, it might be interesting to hang around a spell."

She said that he could have all the coffee he wanted, but that she'd thought he had to go somewhere.

He didn't want to tell anyone he planned to explore some

canyons officially said to be deserted. So he just said he'd ride out soon enough, and lit a cheroot as she went to fetch the pot.

Nobody else came in as it started to get darker out front. By then he'd gotten about all Trisha knew out of her, and she'd started to ask more about him, or about the Henry she now thought she remembered from an earlier trail drive. So he quit while he was ahead and ambled off to see what that saloon might be like.

As Trisha had told him, they did their serious gambling in the card house between the saloon and a ramshackle row of whorehouses around a corner and up a cinder-paved lane. The saloon was the usual twenty-by-forty-foot establishment meant for drinking, conversation, and penny-ante poker. The bar ran back most of the length of the smoke-filled space. There was no piano, and a sign warned everyone to stay out of the back rooms unless they worked there.

Nobody was seated at any of the four tables. At that hour there were only a half dozen cowhands and a jasper in a rusty black suit at the bar. Longarm figured that one for the most nosy. So he bellied up handy to the cuss, but ignored him as he ordered a draft for himself.

The barkeep was usually the one who casually asked a stranger if he was new in town. But this one just poured and didn't seem interested in the change Longarm left on the zinc-topped bar. So Longarm nursed his beer scuttle a third of the way down and lit his second cheroot before he casually said, "Heard some talk about Apache trouble as I was having supper just now."

The rusty suit took him up on it to observe in an agreeable tone, "Noticed the cavalry way you wear your hat. You interested in scouting Apache, Mister . . . ?"

"Crawford, Henry Crawford," Longarm replied easily enough, seeing as Crawford Long had invented painless surgery just in time for the war, and there was that reporter

Crawford of the *Post* who kept writing all that Wild West bullshit about Longarm.

The man in black said he answered to Wesley Jones, and repeated his question about scouting.

Longarm said, "Not hardly. To begin with, the army seems to be out after Victorio along the border way to the south. After that, I'd as soon kiss a sidewinder on the lips as scout Apache. I asked my doubtless foolish question with a view to *avoiding* Apache. I heard something about some having jumped the Jicarilla reserve, is all. Heard some were hiding out in them canyonlands to the east."

The man in black exchanged glances with the barkeep before he quietly asked, "You know your way around La Mesa de los Viejos, you say?"

Longarm replied, "No, I don't. I've never been over yonder, and I ain't sure I'd want to go up one of them canyons with a picnic basket and a pretty gal. Somebody said something about them being *haunted,* and I try to avoid haunts as well as hostile Indians. When I asked about Apache hiding out over yonder, it was only because I got to ride north betwixt the uncertainties of that haunted mesa and the sure-enough Apache reserve to the west."

Wesley Jones said, "So you do. You say you have business up in Loma Blanca or Vado Seguro, Henry?"

Longarm shook his head casually and replied, "I'm bound for Chama. The railroad stop called Chama, not that river out front. Got to meet a business associate there. Just want to make sure I won't run into any other gunplay along the way."

"You say you're headed up to Chama with some gunplay in mind?" the barkeep suddenly blurted out despite himself.

Longarm smiled innocently and said, "Is that how what I said came out? Well, that's one on me. I only meant I had to meet somebody in Chama. A man would have to be a fool to say he was on his way to a gunfight if he was really on his way to a gunfight, wouldn't he?"

The man in black nodded at the barkeep and said, "Don't take my invite wrong, Henry, but there's somebody we'd like you to meet and this saloon ain't where the real action transpires here in town. It's only here on the coach road to serve folks just passing through."

Longarm sipped more suds before he asked with the caution one had to expect from a knockaround rider, "Just what sort of action might you have in mind for this child, Wes?"

Jones, if that was his name, said, "You name it, from faro to fornication, and we'll likely be able to satisfy your cautious nature. Old Mel here can testify to my being a respectable cuss who ain't out to rob you or cornhole you, Henry."

The barkeep nodded soberly and said, "We got our business rep to consider. Old Wes is a gambling man. I'm sorry, Wes, but I got to say it. After that, Mister Crawford, he ain't a *crooked* gambling man. The place of which he speaks is owned by the same respectable lady who owns this saloon and the hardware across the street."

Longarm said that in that case he'd try anything once. So Wesley Jones led him out the back way, past the sign warning them not to pass, and through a maze of back alleyways in the gathering dusk. Then they were in a dimly lit hallway, leading into what looked like the main salon of a steamboat, or the front parlor of a whorehouse.

Then Longarm noticed most of the hired help seemed to be men in suits instead of gals in kimonos, with a rougher-dressed crowd at the bar or around the gaming tables. Jones had been right about the faro. They had crap tables and one of those fancy French wheels of fortune as well. Jones led Longarm over to a red plush sofa and sat him down, saying, "I'll see about our drinks. Don't go away."

Longarm leaned back and lit a cheroot. Jones didn't seem

to be coming back. But after a tedious time another cuss in a black frock coat came over with two gin-and-tonics to ask where Jones was. Seeing as "Henry Crawford" didn't know, he handed him both stiff drinks.

They let him work on them awhile. Longarm set one aside and nursed the other so long that the same cuss came back to sit down beside him and sadly declare, "You're getting to where you need glasses, or else I need to lose some weight and shave off this mustache. You really don't recognize, me, do you?"

Longarm had to admit he didn't. He had a trained eye for faces, and he suspected he knew this routine, having spent some time with a Gypsy fortune-teller who'd really liked it dog-style.

As Longarm stared thoughtfully, the total stranger said, "Come on, who was your best pal in the old outfit?"

Longarm was sure where they were headed now. So he stared hard at his questioner and demanded, "You were in Sibley's Sixth Minnesota? No offense, but my best pals were Swede Bergen and Chad Spooner, and you don't look like either." He took a sip from his glass and added, "Chad got killed later in the Sioux Wars, and you couldn't even be related to old Swede!"

The too-clever-by-half confidence man laughed and said Longarm had been right the first time, going into a song and dance about the not only late, but also nonexistent Chad Spooner having introduced them during a payday crap game. They both laughed and agreed they'd been young and green to shoot craps on an army blanket. It was easy for Longarm to laugh. He'd never been near the Sixth Minnesota during his real war service. He'd learned the little he knew about the outfit the time Billy Vail had sent him to Santee country to look into other Indian trouble. The silly bastard pumping him by pretending to be an old army pal was taking awesome chances, counting on all soldiers having similar memories about crap games, army grub, and mean sergeant majors. But Longarm went along with the game, smart enough to let a wise-ass play him for a fool. The slicker smugly confided, "I've found it wise to change my own name, since I've taken up more sporting ways. I was the kid they called Slim in the third platoon, remember?" It was easy enough to agree. There'd always been some kid called Slim in one platoon or another.

The slicker said, "You and Chad were in the first platoon under old Carlson, right?"

Longarm shook his head and said, "You must be getting *old* too. It was the second platoon and the shavetail was Jergensson."

The so-called Slim nodded eagerly and said, "Gotten fatter, like I said, too. I'd forgot old Jergensson. Whatever happened to the looie after I got wounded and sent home?"

Longarm had no idea, since he'd never served under any Second Lieutenant Jergensson of the Sixth Minnesota, but he managed to look sober as he said, "Stopped a Sioux arrow with his floating ribs up around Yellow Medicine. He wasn't such a bad cuss, for an officer. Say, do you remember that infernal Major Palmer who held a full inspection in that snowstorm?"

It worked. The sneak calling himself Slim decided to quit while he was ahead and got back to his feet. But before he left he had to try. "Your real name was Ferndale, right?"

That Gypsy gal had explained how any wild stab was as likely to get the same response from the mark. So, seeing he was supposed to be the mark, Longarm laughed and said, "Not even close. You must have me mixed up with old Hank Ferguson. I was Hank Bradford before I had to change my name for business reasons."

The trick questioner smiled easily and said, "Right. I'd forgotten old Jergensson too. Smart move to keep your first name and stay so close to the original, Hank. We'll talk about old times later. I got to get back to work before I get in trouble."

Longarm didn't try to stop him. He grinned wolfishly with his smoke gripped in his teeth as he watched the wise-ass circle a table and go through an unmarked door between two red plush curtains.

Longarm rose and drifted over to the nearest faro layout. He didn't place a bet. Faro was as easy to rig as baccarat. But as he watched the dealer's hands the cards seemed to be coming out of the so-called shoe, often a false-bottomed box, about the way a Christian might be expected to deal. So Queen Kirby seemed to be content with straight house odds. The house had to be coming out ahead, though, with a crowd this size.

The man in black who called himself Wesley Jones joined Longarm at the faro layout to demand, "How come you didn't stay put like I told you?"

Longarm softly but firmly replied, "I don't work for you. So who are you to tell me shit?"

Jones smiled uneasily and said, "Never mind. Queen Kirby wants a word with you. Play your cards right and you might wind up working for *her*."

Longarm allowed that he already had a job, but tagged along through that same unmarked door. The big, rawboned redhead seated behind a fancy rosewood writing table was smoking a Havana claro as she waved him to a ridiculous perch on a small plush chair with her bejeweled and manicured left hand, saying, "You'll be pleased to know we sent those others looking for you on their way while you were slugabed and helpless at the hotel, Henry. Why did you tell my boys you were on your way north when you just came from there in a hurry?"

Longarm smiled easily and said, "That's a fool question, if you don't mind my saying so, Miss Queen. Where would *you* tell strangers you were headed if you were riding the owlhoot trail from the north?"

The handsome but hard-looking gal of at least thirty-five summers smiled wearily and said, "Henry, Henry, you haven't changed a bit since last we met and you were trying to fib your way under my way-younger skirts."

Longarm stared hard as he could with a poker face. Staring with a bit more thought, he realized she did look faintly familiar. But he was good at remembering faces, and it was just as likely he was recalling familiar features from different rogues'-gallery tintypes and trying to make a mite more sense out of a mishmash. He tried picturing her with natural hair. That pinned-up henna mop had likely started out brown, to judge from the remains of her more naturally colored plucked eyebrows. Her teeth were a tad pearly for her more timeworn painted face. But if they were false, she'd spent as much on them as she had on her low-cut maroon velvet dress. She likely showed that much bodice so nobody could miss the pearl choker she wore around her neck, as if she was that redheaded Princess Alex of Wales instead of . . . whatever all this was supposed to signify.

She removed the cigar from her painted lips with a smile and said, "After all that sweet talk you don't remember me at all, do you, Henry? I fear Father Time's cruel tricks have been easier on you than me, Henry. But I'll give you a hint. Think back to where you first went after mustering out of the Sixth Minnesota, my young soldier blue."

The hardest part about going along with old fortune-telling shit was resisting the natural impulse to show you weren't really a dumb shit. But Longarm thought fast and declared in a puzzled tone, "I don't recall you from San Antone at all, no offense. It wasn't all that long ago and I'm particular about whose skirts I might or might not mess with. I don't mean you're too ugly even now, but I never mess with gals I'd forget so total afterwards."

She laughed and said, "I'm flattered, I think. You never got that far with me in San Antone, but it was a nice try and I forgive you for never having written."

She waved her cigar at the man in black by the door and continued. "Wes tells me you said you had a job up in Chama. Was that just a lie or was that where you were going when the Townsend boy recognized you and behaved so foolishly?"

Longarm had no way of knowing whether anyone there had ever laid eyes on the real Julesburg Kid. So, hoping he'd thrown them off his back trail with that bluff about San Antone after the war, he patted the action of the Winchester across his lap and replied, "Jason Townsend never recognized me. He said I was the Julesburg Kid. I was still trying to persuade him he had me mixed up with someone more famous when he slapped leather on me. As to what I was really doing in Loma Blanca, or where I was headed from there, it's nobody's beeswax but my own. I ain't asked anyone in this town for a thing I ain't been willing to pay for. I ain't asked anyone anywhere to tell me what *they* might be up to. But seeing we seem to be former sweethearts from San Antone, I'll show you my pee-pee if you'd care to show me your own."

The man in black sucked in his breath, but Queen Kirby laughed and said, "You were playing your cards close to your vest the last time I tried to get some straight answers out of you, Henry. So all right, I'll spread one or two cards face-up for you. To begin with, you're on a fool's errand if you expect to be hired as a gunhand as far north as the D&RG Western stop at Chama. I know what you've heard about a land rush up that way. But I've gotten it from the horse's mouth, or from a BIA official who likes redheads no matter what color hair they have, that the Interior Department's not going to throw all that Apache land up for grabs. There's a lot of Indian policy being debated back in Washington.

The War Department was against moving Apache for no pressing reason to begin with. More than one BIA man doubts the Jicarilla can make do at the Tularosa Agency. But seeing there's been so much other pressure to clear dangerous Indians out of these parts, the Apache are being moved on what Washington calls an experimental basis, with their present reservation held in trust as federal land for at least the next seven years. So what do you think of that, Henry?"

Longarm said, "The Jicarilla may think it's some improvement over losing their land entire. If the BIA allows 'em to return after even one year at Tularosa, they're going to think us white eyes are mighty odd. Their Navaho cousins are still bewildered by the time we made 'em all plant peach trees around Fort Sumner and then let 'em all go home to the Four Corners again. I fail to see why *I* should worry about it, though. Like I said, I go where I please and work for whoever pays me the most."

She said, "We may be able to pay more than any would-be land-grabber, with no Indian land up for grabs just yet. This is where all the real action's about to start, near the south end of that Apache reservation, where the BIA and Indian Police have less to say about things."

"You fixing to grab the south end of the Jicarilla reserve, Miss Queen?" he asked with a deliberately puzzled smile.

The big redhead said, "I'm not in the business of grabbing land. I'm in the business of *owning* land, cattle, and other good things. You should have taken me more seriously that time in San Antone. I may not have aged as gracefully, but I've wound up rich enough to buy and sell all sorts of good things, including men quick enough with a gun to protect me and my property."

"Protect you from whom, Miss Queen?" Longarm asked in a desperately casual tone.

She smiled in a way that might have suggested coyness in

a far more innocent face and said, "We'll talk about it some more, after I've talked about *you* some more with some riders I sent up to Loma Blanca. I expect them back by breakfast-time. If you're what you say you are, I can make it well worth your while to stay here as one of my own Regulators. So if you're really you, you'll do well to stick around."

Longarm nodded and said he'd study on it. As he shifted his weight to rise, she added, "They tell me that skinny blonde waitress at your hotel has been drooling over you, you rascal. I hope you haven't told her all those sweet lies you told me and Lord knows how many of the other girls in San Antone that time. But I take it you'll either be with her in her quarters or up in that hotel room with her should anyone need to get in touch with you tonight?"

Longarm rose to his feet, stiffly saying, "I don't cotton to folks getting in touch with me late at night, ma'am. I'll be where I'll be, and how would *you* like it if I was to blab all over town that it was with *you* instead of a sweet kid who never done you dirty?"

Queen Kirby laughed and said, "I can see why she's drooling over you, Henry. You haven't lost your touch *or* your looks since the war!"

He told her she was pretty too, and allowed that he had to get on back to his hotel. As he left he heard Jones saying, "Told you he'd stood up to your blacksmith for that dishwater blonde. Wouldn't it be fun to be a fly on her bedroom wall tonight?"

Longarm strode through the crowd and out the back door without incident or dawdling. He'd closed one eye along the way so he was able to see outside in the dusk with that one. He ducked into the slot between the card-house and whatever they'd built right next to it. He'd already seen there was no window against the back wall of Queen Kirby's office. It was always better to have a skylight when you kept a card-house safe in one corner. But if there weren't any windows, there was no way anyone could see what he was doing as he dropped to the dirt and rolled under the frame card house. There was the usual eighteen-inch crawl space between the dry soil and overhead floor stringers. He dragged his Winchester after him as he inched on one elbow until, sure enough, he could hear them talking in the office right above him.

Jones was saying something about Apache painting white stripes across their faces from ear to ear. Queen Kirby said, "Never mind about Apache war parties right now, Wes. I asked you what you made of that tall drink of water we were conning earlier. You say he's off the premises now?"

Wes said, "Spider says he just saw him go out the back. You'd better hope we *were* conning him, and not vice versa. Should he be that lawman we were warned about, he's likely heard all the cons of old army pals and long-lost sweethearts."

Queen Kirby laughed lightly and said, "I told you how I mean to make sure. I frankly think he's what he seems, a well-armed and dangerous drifter, looking for action and hearing about that bunch of land-grabbers gathering up by the railroad. Who else would gun a pissant with no warrants out on him, then hang about as if he had more serious business in this territory?"

Wes suggested, "A man with serious business in this territory. As your head barkeep put it together from listening to those Townsend riders in your saloon, that Jason Townsend just started up with our Henry, Longarm, or whoever the blue blazes he really is. Any man, on either side of the law, would have swung his Winchester muzzle up the same way. Fool kid must have thought there was no round in the saddle gun's chamber. But it was still a fool chance to take."

Queen Kirby said, "Spare me the gory details. The point is that a federal deputy should have identified himself to the town law and our mysterious Henry Bradford didn't."

Longarm could picture the man in black shrugging as Wes

replied. "I agree another lawman should have. That's not saying he *would* have if he was in a hurry. Everyone agrees the man who gunned that punk was just passing through. He may have figured he had better places to go in a hurry."

The man they were talking about heard Queen Kirby say, "I just don't know. I'll allow this Henry Bradford, Crawford, or whatever, is a tall tanned galoot with a heavy mustache, wearing his double-action .44-40 cross-draw. I'll allow we were warned the famous Longarm rode out of the Dulce Agency looking much the same, if you'll agree *much* the same ain't *quite* the same."

Wes said, "Your pals with the BIA said Longarm had on jeans and was using a stock saddle in place of his well-known McClellan. You wouldn't need surgeon's hands to punch the crown of a dark brown hat into a different shape, would you?"

Queen Kirby said, "We were wired that Longarm left the Dulce Agency with a pale blue work shirt, a black-and-white paint pony, and a buckskin. My old flame Henry rode in wearing a not-too-new Mex shirt of dusky rose. After that, he's boarding two bay ponies, not a paint with a buckskin, in my very own livery. How do you like it so far?"

Wes said, "Riders have been known to change horses, and those old bays could have been swapped for those better Indian ponies easy!"

Queen Kirby said, "That's why I sent Fats and Tiny up the river to Loma Blanca, Wes. We'll know soon enough whether anyone swapped those Indian ponies for livery nags. I told them to ask if anyone had been wearing a tamer shirt during that saloon fight, too. But I'm going to be mighty disappointed if our Henry really turns out to be Longarm. For they say he's called Longarm because they send him far, wide, and sudden, to be the long arm of federal law."

Wes didn't seem to follow her drift. So she stamped her foot, close to Longarm's ear, and said, "I'm talking about

129

the time even a slowpoke would have taken to get here from the Dulce Agency, you dunce. If that was the real Longarm we just talked to, where has he *been* all this time?"

Wes said, "Somewheres, I reckon. We know he rid out of the Dulce Agency to poke his nose into our own business and—"

"No we don't," Queen Kirby said with a chuckle. "You just heard me tell him about those land-rushers way up the valley. So how you know the real Longarm isn't poking about up yonder, having heard some of *them* are hiring guns, and not having heard a thing about our bigger play down this way?"

Longarm grinned in the darkness right under her feet as he waited for what came next. But all that came next was a bitch from Wes about some stockman who couldn't seem to savvy he was supposed to pay off his gambling markers.

Queen Kirby told Wes not to worry about it, adding she'd own the deadbeat's land and cattle before long in any case. So West asked her about some other business dealings, and Longarm decided to quit while he was ahead.

He rolled out from under the card house and made his way out of there without being spotted in the tricky light of early evening. But even as he headed for the town livery he realized there was no way to take out even one of those bays without Queen Kirby learning he'd gone night-riding. So he headed back to his hotel on foot, his mind in a whirl as he considered whether to risk his ass one way or another. For he had to ride over to that mesa sooner or later, and it sure seemed sooner was best.

His mind made up, he trudged on toward the lamp-lit side entrance, muttering, "Perfidy, thy name is woman, and you're likely to feel a fool when she tattles on you!"

Then he sighed and said, "Aw, shit, stealing a horse would be taking an even bigger chance, and you know you have to get a damned horse off *somebody*!"

He knew Queen Kirby owned neither his hotel nor that dining room.

The dining room was still open and that dishwater blonde seemed pleased to see Longarm. But she told him the kitchen had shut down for the night if he wanted anything more than cooling coffee or a slice of something colder. Seeing there was nobody else out front, he took a deep breath and asked if she thought she could keep some right important secrets that wouldn't mix her up in anything indecent.

She sat him down at a corner table and then sat down beside him, smiling a tad indecently as she confided, "My daddy was a Myers of clan Menzies, and I was raised on the tale of brave Jeannie MacLeod, who refused to say where Prince Charlie was hiding, no matter how the redcoats beat her and raped her!"

Longarm resisted the chance to allow the gal couldn't have enjoyed the beatings and got out his wallet instead as he said, "I need a horse as bad as that old cuss in Shakespeare's play, Miss Trisha. I got the two I rode in with over in Queen Kirby's own livery. Don't see how I'd get either out for some night-riding without them telling her."

The waitress stared thunderstruck at his federal badge and identification as she marveled, "You mean you ain't the Henry Crawford I've been . . . getting to know all this time? Well, I never, and there's the mail coach coming through around midnight if you have to get out of town without anyone but me knowing about it, Henry. I mean, Custis."

He put a hand on her wrist as he put the wallet away, explaining, "Ain't ready to leave for good. Got to snoop around over by La Mesa de los Viejos, and it's too far to walk both ways before sunrise."

She gasped, "You don't want to go over there alone! They say there's spooks, crazy hermits, or just some sickness in the canyon soils. In any case, nobody lives over yonder or *rides* over yonder since the old-timey cliff dwellers all got sick and died a thousand years ago!"

He patted her wrist reassuringly and said, "We heard different. Your government and mine wants me to see just what in blue thunder is really going on over yonder, and like I said, I need a mount to lope me over there and back before dawn. How are we doing so far?"

Trisha said, "Heavens, I don't keep a horse of my own. I've no occasion to go that far from this place I work or my hired cottage down by the river."

She placed her other palm on the back of his already friendly hand. "I'd be afraid to ride out into the open range around town. It was Apache country until mighty recent, and some say Apache riders have been seen out there since!"

Longarm said, "If they were visible to the casual eye I doubt they could have been Jicarilla, Miss Trisha. You don't know anyone you could borrow a mount from, saying you *were* brave enough to ride off somewhere you just had to get to tonight?"

She started to say no. Then she brightened and said, "Meg Campbell! Over by the schoolhouse! She does ride her own pony and, seeing she's from a Highland family as well, we ought to be able to confide in her, Custis!"

Longarm said, "I'd rather we didn't. Two can keep a secret if one of them be dead. A secret shared by three ain't much of a secret to begin with. Couldn't you just tell her some white lie, borrow her pony on the sly, and lend it to me for eight or ten hours, Miss Trisha?"

The waitress thought, sighed, and said, "Lord, I don't know what excuse I'd give for borrowing her pony overnight. She knows I don't have a sweetheart, and she's homely enough to snoop if I told her I'd met somebody since the last time we talked."

Longarm nodded soberly and said, "I wasn't going to ask you to risk your good name. But since you just came up with

132

such a swell excuse, couldn't you say you had to ride out to a big spender's cow spread to admire his stamp collection or whatever? I don't see how your schoolmarm chum could hope to follow you once you borrowed her only mount."

Trisha said, "She wouldn't be able to snoop around any *rancho* I just made up. But she knows where my cottage is and it's only a short walk from her own!"

He shrugged and said, "Nobody would expect to find their pony by any cottage in town if they'd lent it out for a midnight tryst somewheres else, would they?"

Trisha explained, "Meg Campbell's nice, but she's inclined to be nosy. What if she knocked, knowing it wouldn't matter if nobody was there, but meaning to ask me where her pony was if anyone came to the door?"

Longarm started to say she could simply pretend to be out. Then he had a better notion and suggested, "You could hide out in my hotel room whilst I whipped over to the mesa and back."

She slapped the back of his wrist. "Why Custis Long, whatever are you saying?"

He said, "Nothing all that indecent, ma'am. You'll be even safer from my forward ways upstairs alone than here in this dining room holding hands with me. We'll leave the lamp lit and you can read my *Police Gazette* and *Scientific American* whilst I'm out riding. That could even help explain where I spent the earlier parts of this evening, should anybody glance up at my shuttered windows. Might be a good idea if you were to move about and cast some shifty shadows from time to time."

She didn't answer. They sat there holding hands across the table a spell as Longarm gave her the time she needed to make up her mind. Then she did, and she was laughing like a kid starting out on Halloween with some laundry soap and rotten eggs as she said, "Let's do it. It sounds like fun!"

Chapter 12

It wasn't the schoolmarm's cordovan mare pony that gave Longarm a literal pain in the ass. It was the sidesaddle he'd found cinched to the otherwise satisfactory mount when Trisha brought it around to the back of the hotel. The stock saddle he'd borrowed off his male pals at the Diamond K was out of reach in the tack room of the boss lady's livery, and what the hell, it wasn't as if he was hoping to meet up with anyone in the dark. So he handed his room key to Trisha, told her to make sure the door was bolted after her as well, and got on the mare awkwardly with his Winchester across his unusually placed thighs.

Actually *riding* sidesaddle made it tougher for a man to buy all the snickering things other men said about gals who rode that odd way, with the left foot natural in the near stirrup and the other one dangling in midair with one's right knee wrapped around a sort of leather banana sprouting from the forward swells. He doubted a gal could really gallop astride, seated backward with that big banana up inside her. For aside from being too big, the knee brace was set at better than forty-five degrees off center. Longarm found this one braced his right knee well enough for him to lope the mare

134

once they were off to the northeast a ways.

He didn't lope all the way to that mysterious mesa, of course. It was too far for one thing, and too mysterious for another. He reined to a walk when he spied the moonlit rimrocks looming about a mile and a half ahead. He was glad he had when he heard distant hoofbeats.

He hadn't been followed from town. The riders, a plot of riders, were coming his way from the canyon-carved mesa—fast!

Longarm reined off the trail into high, but not high enough chaparral, cussing the old-timers who'd cut all the real firewood this close to town. When the pony balked at moving off farther, Longarm dismounted, Winchester in hand, to lead the balky brute deeper into whatever chaparral was left.

True chaparral, back in Old Spain, was scrub oak. The Mexican and Anglo *vaqueros*, or buckaroos, had decided any sticker-brush too tall to call weeds and too short to call woods was chaparral. The shit all around seemed mostly cat's-claw and *palo verde,* neither offering cover worth mention in bright moonlight unless you'd got a heap of it between you and someone else!

Then he almost stepped off into space, and told the mare he was sorry for cussing it as a balker once he saw why the trail ran the way it did. The arroyo running alongside was so deep he couldn't see bottom. He sighed, got between the pony and the trail, and snicked the hammer of his Winchester to full cock. He knew a man could flatten out in thin chaparral with an outside chance of not being seen. But there was no way to ask a live pony to flatten out like a bear rug, and as long as they were likely to see the damned mare in any case, a man could dodge lead better on his feet. There wasn't a bit of solid cover between his exposed position and the trail.

He could only stand quietly in the moonlight, hoping to pass for a clump of overlooked firewood, as he listened to those riders riding ever closer. Then he could see them in the moonlight, and he cradled his Winchester to cover the pony's nostrils with a palm and held his own breath as well, hoping against hope, even as he knew he had to be hoping in vain.

Then the baker's dozen of bare-headed and cotton-shirted riders had passed by, without a glance in his direction, as the moon shone brightly on white stripes across dark faces framed by long hair bound with rolled cloth. As they jingled off into the darkness he murmured, "Jesus H. Christ, those Quill Indians seem to be headed for *town*! So how do we get there ahead of 'em to raise the alarm?"

The pony didn't answer. Longarm wasn't sure he could have either. Cutting cross-country by moonlight, over busted-up range he didn't know, would be risky riding slow. Those painted Jicarilla had been following the trail at a lope. But hold on. Could no more than thirteen of anything hope to raid a whole town on the prod with all that Apache talk in the air?

He led the pony back to the trail afoot. "They have to be headed somewheres else. In a hurry, seeing they missed us standing there like moonlit graveyard statuary. They could circle the town and be across the river and back on their reserve before sunrise. So that makes more sense."

Then he remounted awkwardly, and rode on up the trail to the northeast as he muttered, "Might be interesting to see where they just *came* from."

He naturally knew better than to ride into a canyon entrance in Apacheria. That could be a fatal move in calmer country. So a quarter mile out, as the range began to rise at a steeper angle, Longarm led the pony off to the other side of the trail, tethered it to lower but less-ferocious greasewood, and gave it a hatful of canteen water before he put the wet Stetson back on his head and started legging it the rest of the way, saddle gun at port arms.

A mesa was called a mesa because that was the Spanish word for a table and the early Spanish explorers had noticed how many flat-topped hills they seemed to have in these parts. Most mesas grew that way because millions of rainstorms had carved away land that hadn't been covered by a lava flow, an ancient lake bottom dried to dense mudrock, or whatever, leaving land that had once lain lower perched higher in the sky. The moonlit caprock of La Mesa de los Viejos was far higher than Longarm had time to climb. So he worked about a third of the way up the gentler slopes below the jagged rim of the flat top, and proceeded to mountain-goat around bends that swung into the canyon that the trail entered down below.

He found he was near the upper limits of easy sidewinding when one of his boot heels dislodged a fist-sized chunk of scree that, fortunately, fetched up in a clump of yucca instead of rattle-clanking all the way down the slope. So he eased down to where the footing felt surer and learned great minds often ran in the same channels when he rounded a bend to spot movement ahead and freeze in place.

He sank slowly down to one knee as he tried to decide what he was looking at, near the very limits of eyestrain in the moonlight. Then one of them stood up to stretch near that big moonlit boulder, and Longarm proceeded to crawfish backward, slow as hell for a white eyes who'd just spotted painted Apache!

He figured they'd been posted there because that boulder overlooked the trail below. He knew he was moving so slowly because you weren't supposed to move at *all* near Jicarilla without getting spotted.

But his luck seemed to hold. It wasn't always clear whether Indians had spotted you or not. Then he'd made it back down to the schoolmarm's borrowed pony, and he'd run it over a mile before he reined in to pat its warm neck, saying soothingly, "I know. You had to have been up there with me to savvy why we left so fast. But let's just set this rise and listen for a spell."

They did, but all Longarm heard was the panting of his mount and the pounding of his own heart. So a million years later he decided they'd best get it on back to town.

He was tempted to lope the spunky mount some more. But he never did. He knew Trisha would have to answer for any needless wear and tear on a borrowed pet. So he trotted it down slopes and walked it up slopes as they made good enough time. They hadn't gone near as far as he'd told Trisha they might. For while a lone lawman might or might not be able to sneak up on outlaws, he wasn't about to try it on Quill Indians in canyon country without a cavalry column backing his play.

They soon saw the lights of Camino Viejo ahead of them, and by now the winded pony was breathing naturally and the dry night winds had blown most of that sweat away. He knew he could get by with just watering it before Trisha took it back if he walked it the rest of the way to cool it down easy. So he did, remembering that cautionary poem about mistreating borrowed horseflesh as they poked along. He recited it to the pony:

"I had a little pony, its name was Dapple Gray.
I lent it to a lady, to ride upon one day.
She whipped it and she lashed it,
She rode it through the mire.
I wouldn't lend my pony, now, for anybody's hire!"

When the pony he was riding didn't seem to notice, he confided, "I've known gals who ride like that. I reckon it's because they let us fool men worry about the rubdowns, whiplash wounds, and loose shoes. But we won't be returning you *too* stove in, considering some of the other little ponies you met on the trail tonight!"

There was no other stock at that hour in the small corral out behind his hotel. But there was water in the trough along the north rails. So he tethered the saddled mare there for the moment, and snuck himself and his Winchester up the back stairs.

Trisha answered his second knock. As he stepped into the dark room she said she'd thought he was gone for the night. So she'd gone to bed. He could see she hadn't wanted to wrinkle her underwear in the very short time it took him to strike a light, say he was sorry, and shake it out. She hadn't seemed quite as blonde down yonder, but few men would have complained. Like a lot of gals who seemed a tad skinny with their duds on, Trisha Myers had a body that would have worked fine cast in plaster for one of those Greek goddess gals.

She stammered, "Shame on you! Or should I say shame on me? I'm all confounded and still half-asleep. What time is it and what did you find out, Custis?"

He rebolted the door and leaned his carbine against the wall, and tried to tell her it was time to get dressed so they could take that pony back. But she somehow sat him down beside her on the rumpled bedding. He said, "It ain't midnight yet, but your schoolmarm chum may be asleep already. So with any luck we'll be able to put her pony safe in its stall out back without disturbing her."

Trisha moved his hand to her bare lap with both of hers as she demurely replied, "Never mind how disturbed Meg Campbell needs to feel right now! I'm so disturbed I've been feeling myself down here, and they say too much of that can make a girl go crazy or blind!"

Longarm put his other arm around her, and stretched them both across the mattress so he could finger her more friendly as they kissed. But when she took his hat off and commenced to fiddle with his gun rig he said, "What about that mare out back?"

To which Trisha replied, bumping and grinding, "Screw the silly pony. Let her get her own swain. Or better yet, screw *me,* for I've not had any since I first came up from Santa Fe last winter and I'm a naturally warm-natured woman, as you may not have noticed."

As a matter of fact he hadn't. But seeing a lady he'd mistaken for a mousy small-town waitress was slithering all over him while she flat out begged for it, he figured it wouldn't hurt that pony to loiter in the moonlight out back for a few more minutes.

Chapter 13

The wise and doubtless French philosopher who'd said no human being is ever more sane than right after they'd enjoyed some good food and a satisfying screw had doubtless met up with someone like Trisha Myers in his travels. Because she'd no sooner come, begging for him to do it faster and swearing she'd kill him if he dared to stop before they were both old and gray, than she commenced to stew about what her friend, the schoolmarm, was going to say if they didn't get her pony back to her before midnight.

Longarm reminded her she'd borrowed the mare for the night, and added it was hardly likely to turn back into one of Cinderella's mice at one minute past midnight. But she pleaded with him to pull his pants back up as she got dressed with an economy of motion that might have inspired rude questions about other hotel rooms from a man less considerate of adventurous blondes.

They encountered nobody else on the dark back streets as they walked the mare to its owner's modest cottage and carriage shed near the more barnlike public schoolhouse. Longarm unsaddled and rubbed down the pony in the darkness of the shed, while Trisha tapped on the kitchen door and had a few words through the slit with a mighty sleepy Meg Campbell, who didn't invite her in.

Trisha rejoined Longarm in the shed, giggling, to report she'd just been called an infernal sex-crazed night owl. Longarm warned her not to hoot too much when her friend woke up all the way and really wanted to know about the other sex-crazed night owl.

Trisha assured him his secrets were safe with her, as long as he meant to escort a lady to her own back door and treat her right.

So he did, and Trisha agreed it was even nicer to just get all the way undressed by candlelight, as if they were old pals, and start all over without the awkward fumblings of that first desperate desire to come before the other one changed his or her mind.

She said she'd never watched herself taking it that way in the mirror before. She said it made her feel like a total whore. But when he said he didn't consider her a whore, she wiggled her tailbone and demanded, "What am I doing wrong, then? You just tell me what any whore has done for you that you liked better and I'll just bet I can do it at least as well!"

He chuckled and assured her, "If you were moving that sweet little ring-dang-doo any better it would hurt. I take it you aspire to become a full-time professional after you've waited tables a tad longer? It's more often the other way around, ain't it?"

She moaned, "Faster! Deeper! I don't want to be a whore who does it with just anybody. But I love to feel like the man I *do* want to do it with considers me a totally depraved slut! My mama always told me girls who really let themselves come were totally depraved sluts!"

"I've heard Calvinist ministers explain why boys and girls were created different," Longarm told her. He didn't ask who'd taught her to finger a man's crack like that as he was trying to move in her with her legs locked around his spine. To prove he understood her better now, and to get her damned finger out of his ass, he withdrew just long enough to roll her over on her bare belly and sweet little cupcakes, shove a pillow under her lap, and enter her some more from behind, with her slender thighs down and almost together as he braced his own knees outside instead of inside her legs to move it in her, as no man had ever moved it in her before, she said, while he planted a bare palm on either of her firm buttocks to shove them open and shut while singing to her:

> "You naughty girl, her mama said.
> You've gone and lost your maidenhead!
> There's only one thing left to do,
> We'll advertise your ring-dang-doo!"

It made her laugh like hell, and then she laughed even louder as she panted, "I'm coming! I'm coming hard and, oh, Custis, it's never, ever, felt so *amusing* before!"

He thought it was fun too. So a good time was had by all, and it made them both feel sad and sentimental when they just had to stop a spell lest they screw one another unconscious.

But neither felt really sleepy just yet. So as they reclined propped up on her pillows and sharing a smoke, Trisha finally recalled how they'd wound up such good friends and asked him, again, where he and her friend's pony had been earlier.

He told her as much as he knew, adding, "Whoever reported a heap of white strangers hiding out amid those old Indian ruins must have been blind. Or else disgruntled Jicarilla have wiped them out and nobody this far from the mesa noticed the considerable gunplay that should have taken place."

She said she hadn't heard about anyone, red or white, camping up in those dry canyons in any numbers. When she asked how he felt about Indians and white renegades being up to something sneaky as hell—in cahoots the way those Mormons and Paiutes had acted out Utah way—Longarm said, "Na-déné ain't Paiute, and the Mountain Meadows Massacre was a sort of ill-considered brawl that nobody had spent all that much time in plotting. The Jicarilla leaders smart enough to plot worth a tinker's dam are up at the Dulce Agency, trying to get as good a deal as they can out of the Great White Father. Disgruntled young bronco Apache don't meditate dark deeds up a canyon with any white outlaws. They kill 'em for their guns and horses."

She took the cheroot from him as she allowed that was the way she'd always heard Apache behaved, too. Billy Vail had never sent *her* down this way to investigate conflicting rumors.

Longarm speculated, "Not much mystery about disgruntled Indians. *I've* often felt disgruntled by our willy-nilly Indian policy, and I must have a better grasp of our two-party system than your average Indian. What can you tell me about numerous new faces in or about these parts, honey?"

Trisha said there were lots of new faces around Camino Viejo, including her own, but that she'd never been up any canyons over by that mesa.

When he asked her what had inspired a gal so fond of . . . nightlife to come up this way from Santa Fe to begin with, she explained she'd heard things were booming up this way, just as the place she'd been working in, near the Governor's Palace in Santa Fe, had been shut down by the new, reform administration.

She said she didn't know why. They'd never told the gals waiting tables out front what went on in the back rooms, but there'd been boomtown talk about a ghost town coming back to life up this way. Hence, here she was.

She agreed with Longarm that Camino Viejo was hardly more than a bigger stagecoach stop than most, with the stage company's local relay station four miles farther on. But she said old-timers said it had been much less before Queen Kirby had come out of the blue to do wonders with her fairy wand, or ready cash.

Trisha explained how the mysterious redhead had swept in one day, three summers back, to find a few forlorn merchants and the slightly more prosperous hotel, serving the crossroads near a river ford and not much else. The Mexicans had been run off years back, and the more stubborn or stupid Anglo homesteaders had eventually found it discouraging to live more forted up, and lose more stock, than folks just a few miles up or down the valley in either direction.

Trisha said, "The way I heard it, Queen Kirby started by buying out a couple of failing *rancheros*, hanging on to their cowboys, and adding some hired guns of her own to make stock-stealing in these parts more threatening to one's health. Then she plowed those profits back into her card house and less wholesome enterprises. Some of the cowboys say there were never all those whorehouses just off the coach road in olden times."

Longarm blew a smoke ring and said, "I was over to her card house earlier. Money can be a lot like snow, once you get a ball of it rolling right. She might or might not have come by her first wad of seed money honestly. I've got no warrant to question that. I fail to see how any federal court would be interested in an old carnival grifter using the profits from one business to start up or buy out another. They call that free enterprise, and I can see how she got her first holding almost free. It was smart to revive a ghost town with a handful of private guns instead of building a town from scratch with a far bigger army of masons and carpenters."

Trisha said Queen Kirby had a building contractor working for her now. "You can't get hardly anything new built here in Camino Viejo without Queen Kirby turning a profit on you. Why did you say she was a carnival grifter? I thought you said you'd never courted her down San Antone way like she said."

Longarm explained, "That was a carnival grifter's trick. I heard about it from another carnival gal one time."

Trish pouted. "A younger and prettier one than Queen Kirby, I'll bet, you rascal!"

He put the cheroot back between her pouting lips as he said soothingly, "You'd win. I thought you admired rascals, you nicely depraved little slut. Be that as it may, everything I know for certain about Queen Kirby smells of popcorn and the tinny blare of a carnival. That might explain her appearing from nowhere with a fast line of patter and a Minnesota bankroll."

That term was a new one on Trisha, despite her sophisicated Santa Fe background. So Longarm explained, "Cheap flash. A Minnesota bankroll is a big bill wrapped around a lot of singles, or even newsprint cut to size. I ain't sure why tinhorns are said to do that more in Minnesota. Heaps of greenhorns there, I reckon. But anyway, once you convince enough folks that you're rich, you can buy heaps of stuff on credit. What you do then depends on how smart a grifter you may be. A tinhorn moves on, owing everyone in town. We call the smarter grifters millionaires, once they mortgage stuff they've bought on credit to get the front money it takes to buy more, and then more, until they don't have to leave town because they own it."

Trisha laughed and said that sure sounded like Queen Kirby. When she asked how he meant to stop the old bawd, Longarm shrugged his bare shoulders and asked, "Stop her from doing what? Nobody's sworn out all that many warrants on Commodore Vanderbilt, Jay Gould, or even Bet-A-Million Gates for grifting their way to fame and fortune."

She said it hardly seemed fair that big fibbers could get so rich by skating the thin ice just within the law.

He said, "I only get to arrest 'em when they break through the ice. The only thing I don't understand about Queen Kirby is why she seems so worried about me. The real me instead of the drifter I told her I was, I mean. For unless she's doing something more crooked than what you just said, she'd have nothing to fear from a federal lawman."

Trisha asked, "What if she's up to something *really* down and dirty?"

To which he could only reply, "That's what I just said."

Chapter 14

Trisha had to be on the job when the morning stage from Santa Fe made its breakfast stop in Camino Viejo. So she was up with the chickens, and served him black coffee and orange marmalade on fried bread, while she had him for breakfast in bed. She allowed that a gal waiting tables tended to nibble all day on the job and skipped sit-down meals if she wanted to keep her figure halfway trim.

They agreed it would hardly be discreet for them to stroll hand-in-hand from her cottage by the dawn's early light. So she left a spell ahead of him. Then he got dressed, rolled over a rear windowsill, and emerged from some crackwillow farther along the riverbank, too far for anybody nosy enough to care.

He mosied back to the hotel, saw nobody had been searching his room, unless they knew his trick involving a matchstick stuck in the door crack under a bottom hinge, and cleaned all three guns on the bed both to kill some time and to make it tougher for folks to kill him.

It took him some time to decide what was making him oddly uneasy as he listened to the morning sounds outside. He hadn't heard anything odd. Birds always chirped and boots always clunked on plank walks in the morning. Then he realized it was sounds he *wasn't* hearing that was odd. Trisha had said a morning stage was due in from Santa Fe. But here it was going on seven in the morning and where was it?

He moved over to the shuttered window overlooking the street and flung the jalousies wide. Things looked quiet for that hour out front. He left his Winchester by the bedstead, locked up, and wedged another matchstick under the bottom hinge before he went downstairs.

He didn't hand over his room key at the desk in the lobby. Nobody really wanted him to while he was still staying there. It was a bother for all concerned to fumble keys in and out of pigeonholes whether a guest was sneaking someone up the stairs or not.

But he stopped there anyway to ask the gummy-eyed desk clerk what time the chambermaid usually made the beds upstairs.

The clerk yawned and asked when he was planning to leave town. When Longarm allowed he didn't know how many more days he might be there, the clerk said the maid would change the damned sheets at the end of the week or whenever he left for good, depending on which came first.

Longarm said, "Don't get your bowels in an uproar, old son. I'd as soon not have anyone popping in and out of my room like a cuckoo-clock bird. That's how come I asked."

The clerk said sullenly that they'd never robbed a guest yet, and asked how many stagecoach strongboxes he'd hidden under the bedstead up yonder.

Longarm smiled and said, "Only one. The coach from Santa Fe seems to be taking her time this morning."

The clerk said, "It ain't running this morning. Apache. Where were you when them riders tore through blazing away to raise the alarm last night?"

Longarm thought hard, nodded, and said, "I do recall what

149

I took for distant thunder along about three in the morning. You say it was something more exciting?"

The clerk said, "You must have been sleeping like a log. They woke me up and I live two streets over. The way I got it, coming to work, was that the Apache raided the Chandler spread just north of town. Lucky for the Chandlers, the crew at the stage relay up the road heard the whooping and shooting and came to help. But the fool Apache shot out all the window glass, turnt over the shithouse, and naturally run off all Bob Chandler's riding stock."

Longarm whistled softly and said, "I wonder if the army knows as much as we do about all this."

The clerk shrugged and said, "They've wired Santa Fe. Wires to the north have already been cut. But at least they won't butcher the folks aboard that morning coach, and the one coming down from that railroad stop at Chama won't even start, seeing the wire's down in Apacheria."

As Longarm turned to stride out front, the clerk added in an oddly cheerful tone, "The army's got all its spares chasing old Victorio along the border right now. They ain't about to detach even a squadron to chase Jicarilla horse thieves. We have to lose us some hair up this way before the soldiers in blue show up."

Longarm was afraid he agreed. He headed for the Western Union on the corner anyway. Billy Vail had sent him on a wild-goose chase. There were no outlaws holed up in the canyons of that mesa. Not alive, at any rate. But meanwhile, some Jicarilla kids were fixing to get their whole nation in a whole heap of trouble if somebody didn't do something about it before white blood was spilled!

Knowing there was no way to wire BIA headquarters in his official capacity without giving his true identity away, Longarm strode into the combined tobacco stand and telegraph office to send a wire east via the line to Santa Fe. But the older gent who sold cigars more often than he sent wires anywhere, morosely informed Longarm he was solely in the tobacco business that morning.

"Apache," he laconically observed, figuring nobody but a tenderfoot needed more explanation than that when Western Union shut down for repairs in Apacheria. Nobody had ever had to explain electricity to any hostiles. All they'd had to hear was that the blue sleeves got word somehow along those singing wires stretched from pole to lonely pole, far from the gaze of any cavalry patrol.

With the wires down in all directions, Longarm felt no pressing need to identify himself as he stocked up on some cheroots instead.

As he stepped out on the walk, pausing to light one of the cheroots, the man in black called Wesley Jones caught up with him. "Where have you been? They just told me you weren't in your room and I've been looking high and low for you!"

Longarm finished lighting his cheroot and shook out the match before he said, "You found me here instead because I was running low on tobacco. What did you want with me, Wes?"

Jones said, "It's Queen Kirby who'd like another word with you. I was asking where you might have been earlier this morning when she first sent me to fetch you."

Longarm blew smoke in the rude questioner's face and calmly told him, "Where I might or might not have been is my own beeswax. When did Miss Queen adopt me as her wayward child? I can't come up with any other reason I'd have to report to her for roll call. Can you?"

Jones said, "I can. You can't ride on to that job up Chama way with Apache on the warpath. Meanwhile she's got as good if not a better job for a man who's not afraid to use a gun on short notice."

Longarm didn't want too seem too anxious. On the other hand, he sure wanted to know why Queen Kirby was recruiting a private army of hired guns. So he shrugged and said, "I'll hear her out. I ain't saying I want to work for any woman, though."

The man in black smiled thinly. "You'll find Queen Kirby as tough as most he-bosses if you cross her. Now that it's over, I can tell you just how close you came last night to finding out how tough she can get. How come you swapped two fine Arab ponies for bay scrubs up Loma Blanca way, Crawford?"

Longarm was glad he'd picked an alias easy to remember as he answered casually, "I left in a hurry. Would you want to be riding a cream and leading a palomino right after a serious gunfight, Wes?"

The man in black led the way along the walk as he chuckled and replied, "They say you changed your shirt from green satin to rosy cotton, too. I admire a man who thinks fast on his feet. It's a good thing you never put on a pale blue shirt or swapped those pale ponies for a buckskin or a paint."

Longarm knew exactly what he meant, but naturally pretended not to as they walked on past that saloon and around to the card house, where this morning better than a dozen ponies were tethered out front.

When they went inside, the gaming room was full of tobacco smoke and some hard-looking gents, armed to the teeth and not playing cards or shooting craps. When Longarm commented that it looked as if someone was fixing to go to war, Jones told him he was right.

They went into Queen Kirby's office. A hatchet-faced individual with an old army shirt, shotgun chaps, and an English Enfield .476 six-shooter was leaning against a back wall, arms folded Indian-style. Queen Kirby asked, "You ever meet up with Poison Welles before, Henry?"

Longarm stared, neither friendly nor unfriendly, at what he assumed to be the stranger instead of a desert water hole, and allowed he'd never had the pleasure.

Queen Kirby said, "Fortunately for us all, Poison here knows the famous Custis Long, or Longarm, on sight."

Poison Welles nodded soberly and declared, "He ain't half as tough as they say he is in the *Rocky Mountain News*. I backed him down in Durango, just about this time of the year, around '76 or '77. Thought he could dance with my gal just because he was a famous lawman. But when I told him to fill his fist, he just grinned like a fool and said he'd only been funning."

"I'm sorry I missed that," said Longarm, trying not to sound too sarcastic. He wasn't supposed to be as clever as Queen Kirby, and it was no skin off his nose if she didn't know the town of Durango hadn't *been* there in '76 or '77, since they'd built it on land the Ute had lost more recently, after that ill-advised Meeker Massacre closer to White River. He didn't know why fabulists like Poison Welles made up such whoppers, but he was glad this one had when Queen Kirby said, "We'd already backtracked you enough to feel we were safe in calling you Henry, Henry. But having Poison here assure us you can't be who you couldn't be means I may as well lay some more cards on the table, face-up. I want you and your gun hand working for me, Henry. I'm paying a hundred a week and found, with a bonus for each and every time you really have to fire a gun. How do you like it so far?"

Longarm quietly asked, "Who might I be fixing to gun for you?"

She said, "Right now I've got Apache pestering me. I knew from the beginning that that stupidity with the Jicarilla was going to cause more Indian trouble. Those fools down in Santa Fe never thought ahead as they were pulling strings to move the Jicarilla. I told you what the wise-money boys told me about the Bureau of Land Management freezing all that Indian land, and now we're stuck with upset Indians, at a time the army can't spare us any help with them!"

Longarm cocked a brow and cautiously asked, "You've been recruiting gunhands to fight *Indians*, ma'am?"

She shrugged her bare shoulders and replied, "Somebody has to. I just told you the army seems too busy. General Sherman says he just can't spare the troops to chase horse thieves when Victorio and his four hundred total savages are running wild down south."

She took a drag on her cigar before adding primly, "I prefer to call you boys my' Regulators,' not my hired guns. I can assure you all it's perfectly lawful, Henry. I've cleared it with both Santa Fe and our county sheriff up Ensenada way. So how's about it?"

Longarm exchanged glanced with Poison Welles, as if he thought the blowhard knew his ass from his elbow, then turned back to Queen Kirby to demand, "What's the bounty per Apache head, ma'am?"

She met his gaze unflinchingly and said, "I knew you were my kind of gun, Henry. A hundred dollars on each dead buck and fifty for a squaw or kid. We don't take prisoners. Any Apache who messes with *me* will learn I'm not a fool government you can fight with one day and tap for a handout the next."

Longarm nodded soberly and said, "I follow your drift, ma'am. I've often wondered why Uncle Sam fights 'em in the summer and feeds 'em through the winter, myself. But ain't we likely to get in trouble with said government, slaughtering wards of said government without a hunting license?"

Queen Kirby shrugged and said, "Hell, I'm only asking you to *shoot* the red devils for me. Nobody's asking you to sleep with them or buy them any drinks."

Poison Welles chimed in. "White folks got the same right as anyone else to defend themselves, and it's the Apache, not us, as started it!"

Longarm didn't feel like debating that point. He'd warned Indians more than once not to give his own kind the excuse to fight them if they weren't ready to start their own industrial revolution.

He said, "Well, like Wes here says, I'd never get up to Chama to see about that other job alone at a time like this. So I reckon you just hired another gun, Miss Queen."

She said, "Good. Go home and get your Winchester. Then saddle up any mount in my livery and be ready to ride. I've heard those Apache are holed up around La Mesa de los Viejos and I want you to lead the patrol, Henry. For I know you're a killer and I want those damned Apache killed, right down to the last papoose!"

Chapter 15

Longarm didn't intend to kill anyone he didn't have to. But a reservation-jumping Jicarilla could offer mighty persuasive arguments for killing him wherever you might meet him off his reservation. So Longarm was not too upset to find that one canyon deserted once he'd led, or at least rode out ahead of, Queen Kirby's score and a half of "Regulators."

The riders he'd spotted the night before had been camped among some barely noticeable ruins. The "Old Ones" of La Mesa de los Viejos had either dwelt there mighty far back, or built their cliff dwellings and canyon-bottom pueblos mighty carelessly.

They'd all dismounted to scout for sign amid the squares or circles of freestone. So Longarm was counting flies on some horse apples by what might have been a kiva, filled in and almost totally erased by the rare floodwaters of many a year, when the famous badman Poison Welles came over to join him, holding a fresh but empty tin can.

Poison said, as if he knew, "Canned salmon. No Apache ever brung *this* from his agency. Reservation trading posts don't stock any sort of canned fish for Apache."

Longarm took the can and sniffed it, saying, "Been open and empty a spell. Might have been whites up this way ahead of 'em. I heard in town that some kid had seen a mess of white strangers over by this mesa a spell back. You hear anything about that, Poison?"

Welles shrugged and replied, "No white boys up this way right now. No Indians neither. But wouldn't you say them turds at our feet were dropped by a white man's horse?"

Longarm nodded and said, "I was just admiring the oat husks. The flies say the pony was here about two days back. The Pueblos never named them Apache because they steal from one another."

Poison Welles said, "I follow your drift, but they raided that white outfit last night, not two days ago."

Longarm made a mental note to be careful with Poison Welles in spite of that bad first impression. The West was full of pests who seemed half bullshit and half real. Old Bill Cody had started to grow his hair shoulder-length and wear fringed white buckskins like some of those sissy boys who stayed in camp with the women. But it was still a fact that he had shot all those buffalo, and had fought it out blade-to-blade with Yellow Hand of the Cheyenne Nation.

Wesley Jones, another bullshit artist, came over to ask what was going on. Longarm said, "Mixed signals. Red or white campers this far up the canyon. I'd go with white if I didn't have good reason to, ah . . . suspect a good-sized war party rode out of this very canyon just last night."

Jones said, "Damned gravel makes it hard to track any breed at all, not to say which way or when, Hank. What inspired you to say Apache in particular were up this way last night?"

Longarm reminded himself that Cockeyed Jack McCall had been taken for a harmless blowhard till he'd really gone and gunned Wild Bill in the Number Ten Saloon. Then he chose his words carefully and told them both, "I can't say I saw them with my own two eyes. But don't it stand to reason? Why would any white boys with a lick of sense be way out here in this dry canyon during an Apache scare when they could be safely drinking rotgut or, hell, sipping cider over by the river in Camino Viejo?"

Poison Welles stared around at the canyon walls as he objected. "I can't see Indians camping even dumber, Hank. This is about the last stretch of canyon I'd expect to find an Apache camp."

Jones scuffed at the outline of an old stone wall with his boot and said, "Oh, I dunno. You can see *some* Indians must have favored this spot in olden times."

Poison Welles shook his head, wigwagging his comical tan Texas hat, and insisted, "Anasazi lived up these canyons on sites and for reasons no modern mind can fathom. But Apache are worse than schoolboys about graveyards and haunted houses, which these old ruins sort of combine. Could you see kids scared of ghosts camping out in a graveyard when there was plenty of sites just as good further up or down?"

Longarm managed not to ask how a man who knew that much about Indians could fail to know the town of Durango had mushroomed on a recent hunting ground. He said instead, "We know what's down this canyon we just came up. Let's go on up it some more and have a look-see."

As they strode back to the others and their ponies, the hard-to-figure Poison Welles called ahead, "We're moving on. But don't nobody mount up. It's safer to walk your horse around a canyon bend in Indian country."

A prouder man might have reminded Welles that Queer Kirby had told *himself* to lead the patrol. But Longarm let it go, letting Poison have as much rope as he wanted.

The canyon boxed a furlong farther on. That explained the ancient ruins at ground level. Noah's forty days and forty nights would have had a tough time flooding the canyon floor this close to its upper end. The box was paved with gravel, too, along with scattered horse turds. This time it was Jones, despite his soft hands and carnival grifter's manners, who declared, "They must have kept their Indian ponies up here in this natural corral."

Longarm said, "Somebody's ponies at any rate. But they ain't here now, and there must be more canyons than this one cut into the mesa."

There were. It took the better part of the day, with some volunteers scaling the rocks to scout around with a buzzard's-eye view, before Longarm and all his so-called Regulators decided there weren't any fool Indians to be found around La Mesa de los Viejos now.

They reported back, hot and dusty, only to be told another spread had been raided, this time down the river to the south, with the wire still down and nobody moving along the coach road.

When Longarm said you traveled through Apacheria by night but hunted Apache by day, because that was the best time to find them holding still, Queen Kirby told them all to get a good night's rest and go *get* the savage rascals at sunrise before they hurt somebody.

Longarm enjoyed a good meal, a hot bath, and even got some rest before Trisha got off work and rejoined him in his hotel room.

After he'd shown her how much he'd been missing her too, she asked how long he'd be staying there in Camino Viejo.

He finished lighting their cheroot, patted her bare shoulder, and truthfully replied, "Can't say. If those mysterious white strangers were ever holed up around that mesa, they ain't there now. I might have gone riding with some of them today. Queen Kirby seems to have all the gunslicks in these parts on her payroll. I'm still trying to figure out why."

She took a drag, handed the smoke back and said, "I was working in Santa Fe when they hired all those Regulators down in Lincoln County. But we sure heard about all the feuding and fussing. You don't suppose Queen Kirby is out to murder the county sheriff and just take over like a *real* queen, do you?"

Longarm said, "The lady don't seem that stupid. The Lincoln County War was mutual stupidity, no matter what you read in the papers about it. The Murphy-Dolan faction thought they owned a whole county because Major Murphy said so three times, like that queen Miss Alice met up with in Wonderland. The Tunstall-McSween side said *they* owned Lincoln County because Truth, Justice, and Billy the Kid was on their side."

He took a drag on the cheroot and said, "It was a bare-knuckles fight betwixt stubborn cusses who, all huddled together, might have added up to one mature adult. Old John Chisum sided with Tunstall and McSween at first. But being a grown-up, he backed out in time and wound up way better off when . . . Hmm, I wonder if Queen Kirby noticed that."

Trisha began to fondle him fondly as she repressed a yawn and asked, "Was that the Chisum they sing about in that trail song, hon?"

He said, "Nope. Jesse Chisholm blazed that cattle trail north from Texas. John Chisum is the biggest cattle king in New Mexico Territory now. Because he had the brains to pull in his horns and sit it out as the Gingham Dog and Calico Cat ate each other up. You can't just shoot folks, rob them of their land and property, and sit there like a fool dog with a bone, no matter how wild Ned Buntline writes about these parts. The Murphy-Dolan boys gunned Tunstall and McSween in turn, only to have their tame Sheriff Brady back-shot and have martial law declared by the new governor appointed by President Hayes. Jimmy Dolan ran off, along with most everyone else who meant to go on living outside of jail, or simply go on living. Old Murphy died broke, his business ruined by the war and his health ruined by all the nerve tonic he'd been taking in increasing doses. Some say The Kid is washing dishes down at Shakespeare, near the border. I don't know where he might be right now and don't much care. He's only wanted local for gunning Sheriff Brady. My point is that everyone got ruined but Uncle John Chisum. When it was all over he was in position to buy up all that property mortgaged or abandoned by the fools who'd ground one another down to nothing, see?"

She began to stroke it harder as she demurely replied, "I guess so. But there only seems to be one side around here. There's Queen Kirby and those Indians she wants you boys to get rid of for us all. No white folks around here are at feud with Queen Kirby, and the Indians don't have any property anyone can grab without the government's say-so, right?"

He snubbed out the cheroot and rolled back on top of her as he decided, "That's about the size of it. But I'll be switched if I can see anyone hiring her own well-paid army to fight Indians *pro bono*—meaning a free public service in lawyer talk."

Then he was too busy to talk, and she wouldn't have been listening in any case, as they both went deliciously loco some more.

Chapter 16

The next few nights were as nice, or nicer, with Trisha proving a real sport about experimenting in bed or anywhere else he could think of. But the days went tedious as hell, with those infernal raiders neither moving on to fresh fields of action nor offering a stand-up fight. It was almost as if the painted rascals were out to taunt the white eyes in and about Camino Viejo; for they seldom hit more than half a day's ride in any direction, and always seemed to double back and hit some more every time it seemed they'd ridden on.

Everybody Longarm talked with seemed as bewildered, whether they worked for Queen Kirby or her neighbors. Some were more jealous than others, but nobody was or really bitter terms with the hard-faced but jovial redhead.

Some Western Union riders repaired the wire to Santa Fe. It was cut somewhere else the same day, as if the Indians had been watching.

Longarm watched for smoke signals as he led patrols out on both sides of the river, trying in vain to cut the Indians' trail, with just enough sign hither and yon to let you know they were still around without saying exactly where.

Then it got worse. Wes Jones, leading his own patrol south along the riverbanks, came upon what was left of old Pappy Townsend and the bunch he'd led all the way to Santa Fe and back in search of the man who'd gunned their young kinsman Jason up at Loma Blanca. When Jones brought them back, stacked like bloated cordwood on a buckboard, it was generally conceded they'd have been far better off staying up in Loma Blanca. One could only hope the bodies had been stripped and carved up that thoroughly after they'd been killed.

Queen Kirby ordered eight pine coffins in a hurry for the bunch of them, and sent them on their way north, more dignified if not a whiff sweeter-smelling under the sunny New Mexico sky.

When he told Trisha about it later, the pale blonde turned paler and said she was scared, which sounded reasonable. Then she pleaded with him to take her away from such savage surroundings, which he would not, he told her, because he wasn't fixing on going anywhere before he learned what was going on.

They were getting undressed at the time, of course, so she tried to take unfair advantage of him, on her knees beside the bedstead, as she said, "Pooh! You told me you were a lawman, not the hired hand of a silly old thing whose only crime is that overdone henna rinse! You told me just the other night that neither gambling nor whoring are federal offenses, lucky for us, and *everybody* shoots to kill at Apache, save for the army."

He sighed and said, "I've noticed that. Some officers seem to go along with the Indian policy of the moment, whilst others like to preserve the species, lest a son still in West Point graduate to find no hostiles of his own to hunt. I sometimes feel we'd have been kinder in the long run to follow the Mexican or Canadian Indian policies. I know it saves a heap of money to just leave Indians be when they ain't bothering nobody, and arrest them as outlaws when they are."

She didn't answer. She couldn't talk with her mouth so full. He lost interest in what was going on everywhere else on earth that night.

It was downstairs in the dining room the next morning, her serving him more sedately with ham, eggs, and an innocent expression, when he told her, "Don't pack your bags just yet. But I reckon I could get us out of here aboard my two livery nags by way of the far side of the river and up to the railroad inside the reservation line. I doubt like thunder we'd meet many reservation-jumpers on or about the reservation they'd jumped. So by now nobody else over yonder should know whether to be sore at me or not."

She looked so puppy-dog eager he quickly added, "Hold on. I never said I'd be able to carry you all the way back to Denver with me, and I ain't even fixing to cross the river till I check just a few more angles out."

She bent over to pour him more coffee as she asked what else there could be to find out about a sort of informal but sensible enough way to cope with any sort of wild and woolly killers.

He said, "We've been whittling away at where those raiders could be holing up by day to raid at night. But like you said yourself, fighting Indians for fun and profit ain't my regular occupation."

None of the few others having breakfast seemed to be listening, so he confided, "I just want to wire some questions hither and yon about old Queen, her boyfriend Wes, and a couple of her other old boys. She and the one who says he used to be called Slim tend to sound like a pair of carnival barkers when they get into a two-sided conversation. They lard their jargon with so many terms I can barely understand, and I've spent some time with carnival folk."

She pouted. "I was wondering where you learned to contort a poor girl into such dirty positions. Is that what you're

164

planning to do to that old redhead as soon as you get the chance?"

He laughed incredulously and said, "Not hardly, albeit she does remind me of somebody prettier from a time gone by. I've been busting brain cells trying to remember. Neither of us would have forgotten a long-ago love affair, despite her bull about having met me before in San Antone."

Trisha said, "Goody! Does that mean you'll still let me French you if we meet like this a dozen years from now?"

He sighed and said, "Honey, you can do that when I come back to you this very evening, should that be your pleasure as well. Meanwhile, I think I may have seen a younger Queen Kirby's face on a tintype or sepia-tone. It's possible she resembles some male relation on file. In either case, that carnival or theatrical background may narrow the target area down. I know some theatrical agents I can call on and, of course, the Pinkertons keep files on grifters, bunko artists, and such, because they provide security at so many state fairs and such."

Trisha had to go serve somebody else. He didn't care. He'd only been musing aloud with the only person he could trust with his musings in these parts.

He finished breakfast and ambled over to the card house. Queen Kirby and her Wesley hadn't shown up yet. Longarm had learned the others called the man in black *her* Wesley after hearing some shocking comments by old boys who'd overheard sloppy noises through door panels from time to time.

Longarm hadn't asked for further details. It was enough to know who might be making sloppy noises with whom. Everybody acted sort of disgraceful at such times, and some said the real queen, Victoria, favored that Scotch butler, John Brown, because it saved time behind closed doors with the two of them wearing skirts.

It was more important to know Wes outranked Darts Malloy, the wise-ass who'd said they'd known one another as Hank and Slim in the old Sixth Minnesota. He sure *talked* like a gent who'd once run a dart game in some dingy traveling show, though he rode well enough.

Queen Kirby finally came in, looking flushed and out of breath, as if she'd been out jumping fences sidesaddle. Old Wes, coming in after her looked as if he'd been doing some riding that morning as well.

Queen Kirby declared, "We've been talking it over. We have to do something about those blamed Apache. It seems pretty clear it's not such a big war party and that they're shifting around like spit on a hot stove."

When nobody argued she said, "I want you boys to split up into smaller patrols to cover more range. How small can we get away with, seeing you're our Indian expert, Henry?"

Longarm soberly observed, "George Armstrong Custer was an Indian expert, Miss Queen. He wrote the training manuals the army still uses, and we know he didn't have enough men with him at Little Bighorn. But I reckon corporal's squads, every man with at least a fifteen-shot Henry, ought to be able to handle the baker's dozen we seem to be chasing all over creation."

She seemed confused by the numbers. Darts Malloy volunteered to her, "Corporal's squad is eight riders, Miss Queen. Baker's dozen is thirteen. Me and Henry were in the army together and that's the way you talk in the army. Ain't that right, Henry?"

Longarm dryly answered, "If you say so, Slim. If each head scout gets to pick and choose, I reckon I'd like to try those canyons off to the northeast today. Nobody's been back since we spotted sign over yonder days ago."

Nobody argued and Longarm didn't care who wanted to tag along as long as they were packing fifteen rounds in their magazines and one in the chamber. Most Indians packed

166

single-shooters, or at best, the seven-shot Spencer repeaters the BIA had gone on issuing in fair weather or foul—to hunt with, of course. You could really nail a rabbit with .52-40 Spencer round.

He rode out with his own eight Regulators a few minutes later, mounted astride one of the boss lady's better ponies, in this case a blazed roan with white socks. Darts Malloy, alias Slim, and Poison Welles seemed to want to hunt Apache with him. As they all rode out, Longarm noticed four of the others were on joshing terms with old Poison. The others seemed to have been with Queen Kirby longer. Longarm didn't trust any of them as far as he could spit against a windstorm.

But they got up to the mesa without incident. Longarm allowed, and Poison Welles agreed, that any Jicarilla lookouts peering down at them from the rimrocks should have sent up some smoke by this time. It made Longarm less sure of himself to have a dime-novel enthusiast agreeing with him on Indian-scouting tactics!

They dismounted near the mouth of that one promising canyon and Longarm went first afoot, leading the roan with his cocked Winchester pointing ahead. They'd almost made it as far as those nearly gone ruins when Darts Malloy pointed at the rocks across the way and said, "Say, don't that look like some sort of cavern betwixt them big boulders?"

Longarm had to stare hard before he made out what surely seemed an opening in the sandstone. He muttered, "That's what I get for a snap judgment. You've got good eyes, Darts. I'd best have a peek. Would you hold these reins for me, Jennings?"

He handed the reins to the nearest willing hand and moved in on the dark opening, saddle gun at port. He hadn't told anyone to stay or follow. He was mildly annoyed when he heard Darts telling the others to stay put while he and his old army pal saw what was inside that hole in the wall. But it did make as much sense to have somebody covering their backs, and the cleft was barely wide enough for the two of them single file.

It seemed to be more a natural crack, widened by erosion, than a tunnel or adit carved with any purpose in mind. Then he spied the scattered chalky bones in the gloom ahead and declared, "No Jicarilla born of mortal mama would ever hide shit in here! See those skulls? Looks like a family tomb from years gone by. I make it a daddy Anasazi, a mama Anasazi, and look at all those baby Anasazi!"

Then he heard someone yelling, "Longarm! Down!" and so he was already dropping to the gritty bone-strewn floor as all hell busted loose in the confined space.

He could only hug the dirt and hold his own fire as bullets and rock fragments spanged off the rock walls above him and the air got stuffy with black powder smoke. Then somebody flopped limply half on top of him, and as Longarm rolled him off and over he could just make out the surprised dead face of his old army pal Darts Malloy.

The shooting had stopped. Longarm eased his own weapon in position across the handy corpse and sat tight until a familiar voice called out, "You still with us, Longarm?"

The bewildered federal man replied, "Who wants to know?"

The rider he'd known up until then as Poison Welles called back, "Rod Duncan, New Mexico Territorials. Your old army pal was about to shoot you in the back just now. Lord knows how he meant to explain it. Maybe he figured he wouldn't have to. My boys threw down on his boys as soon as I opened up on the sneaky bastard!"

Longarm asked a trick question about the Governor's Palace down in Santa Fe. When Poison, or Duncan, confessed he'd never heard tell of a stenographer called Rosalinda, Longarm got to his feet and waded out through the gunsmoke to regard a mighty grim tableau around the sunlit entrance.

One of the two thoroughly shot-up cadavers was still crapping blood and worse in slow but steady spurts. The other poor bastard just lay there.

The other lawman, who'd ordered the surprise ending to Malloy's wicked plan, nodded at Longarm and asked, "How do *you* figure all of this, pard?"

Longarm smiled thinly and said, "They had orders to kill me. What I really find mysterious is how a paid-up Apache fighter ever came up with Durango being there back in '76!"

Duncan shrugged and said, "Wes Jones was asking if anyone there had ever met the one and original Longarm. I'd read that story about you being in Durango *some* damned time and figured it would help if I volunteered. To tell the truth, I don't know Colorado as well as I know New Mexico."

Longarm asked, "How come you joined up ahead of me, Rod?"

The New Mexico lawman indicated his four modestly smiling associates as he explained, "We all did. Governor Wallace ordered us to when he heard something odd was going on up this way. I've been hoping you might know. I'll be damned if I can make any sense of it."

Longarm said, "Neither could I, until just now. Let's leave these old boys here for now and go make us some arrests. I'll explain along the way."

Duncan asked, "What about them Indians?"

Longarm said, "Ain't no Indians. Soon as you figure *that* out the rest just follows as the night the day!"

Chapter 17

It was mid-afternoon when Longarm and his five fellow lawmen reined in near that saloon in Camino Viejo. They stopped there first because Longarm recognized the pretty Morgan mare Wesley Jones had ridden out on, tethered with a half dozen more to the saloon's hitch rail.

The man in black, now dusty as well, seemed to be holding court at the table farthest back. The seven or eight others with him were all on their feet and, recognizing Longarm and the man they knew as Poison Welles, made way for them.

Jones rose to his feet, smiling uncertainly as he said, "Not a sign of Apache off to the south this time. I see you boys got back early too. How'd you make out?"

Longarm soberly replied, "Darts Malloy is dead. So are Jennings and Alderthorpe."

Jones gasped, "My God, what happened? You brush with them Apache?"

Longarm said, "Nope. Let's talk about them Apache. Jicarilla on the prod and off their usual range who don't have any lookouts posted to smoke-signal our own movements as we tear-ass all over after 'em."

Jones said, "Well, we've been figuring them for kids, acting on their own with no serious chiefs in charge."

Longarm smiled thinly and said, "That's likely why they rode past a grown man and his mount standing in the open by the light of the silvery moon. That's likely why they'd been camped, or paused to put on their costumes, in a haunted canyon. I have it on good Jicarilla authority that the mere sight of what they call a *chindi* will kill you on the spot after dark. Yet there they were, eating fish cold from the can without any camp fire, smack dab on top of an Anasazi ghost town. It makes one wonder, don't it?"

Jones tried. "Hell, if the fool Apache were acting usual we'd have caught up with 'em by this time, right?"

It was Rod Duncan who quietly observed, "One would certainly think so. Me and a couple of these other old boys have scouted Jicarilla in the past. They were out in force as late as '73. Yet try as we might, we could never cut the rascals' trail. It's been my own experience that when experienced trackers can't find anybody to track, there's nobody to track."

"Or there's somebody *else*," Longarm amended, adding, "We naturally never tracked sign left by other Regulators far enough to mention. So who do you reckon scared all them local settlers, and even butchered a bunch of riders from other parts, to set a good example for those in *these* parts who might not have been scared enough yet?"

Jones licked his lips and stepped back to give himself more room as he stammered, "How do you expect *me* to answer for the loco ways of infernal Apache, Henry?"

Longarm said, "Aw, come on, you know who I am. You've known since the first day your boss hired me. But lucky for me, neither of you spotted Inspector Duncan here for anything but a harmless blowhard you could use as a tool."

Then he said, "As for why we'd like you to answer some questions about them fake Jicarilla, it's obvious as hell you were them!"

The man in black was good. He dropped to the floor and tipped the table on its side between them as he went for his side arm. Longarm drew and fired four rounds at the bare pine tabletop. It took more than an inch of pine to stop two hundred grains of lead backed by forty grains of powder. But the results were far from neat as Jones stopped the deformed slugs, and a heap of pine slivers, with softer flesh.

Meanwhile Duncan and his own boys were backing Longarm's play with blazing guns of their own. For naturally the hirelings who'd been riding directly under Jones had as much to answer for, and hoped to beat the hangman's noose with gunplay of their own.

They lost, of course, with one of Duncan's boys pinked along one rib by a bullet, and all but the barkeep and another man on the other side dead. The one survivor had been as quick as the barkeep when it came to reaching for that pressed tin ceiling. So he was doubtless good for a signed statement.

Chapter 18

Duncan had instructed his own deputies to head off other Regulators as they rode in and either arrest or deputize them pro tem, depending on whether they'd been riding at certain times with the late Wesley Jones, alias Frenchy O'Donnel, or, like most of the outfit, just going through the motions as tools of the boss lady. So just Duncan and one of his deputies tagged along as Longarm strode on to the card house to confront Queen Kirby.

The big redhead must have heard the noise, judging from the way she greeted them, seated in her office behind that writing table as the one back-up man positioned himself just outside the door to make certain they weren't disturbed.

Queen Kirby smiled weakly and asked, "What's going on? Why are you staring at me that way, Henry?"

Longarm said, "You know who I am and I sure feel silly about that. You'll be pleased to hear your lover boy never gave you away as he lay oozing his last just now. But Thornhill gave up without a fight, and as soon as he confessed he'd met up with you all on the carnival trail, it all came back to me where I'd seen your pretty face before. You always have liked to make total fools of mere mortal men, haven't you, Dolly Moore? You've come a long way since you had that freak show back in Saint Lou. Don't *do* that, Dolly!"

But a monstrous Le Mat revolver was already rising from behind the writing table in a jewel-encrusted hand. So Longarm fired point-blank with the derringer he'd had palmed just to be on the safe side. And that red wig flipped skyward as the now gray-headed Queen Kirby, or Dolly Moore, flew backwards with the chair and all, in a flurry of velvet and scattered pearls.

As the smoke still hung above the writing table, Longarm moved around it for a better look, grimaced, and said, "Takes a spine shot to snap their heads back that hard. Dead as a turd in a milk bucket. But we've got that fairly full confession and some of the others may fill in a few gaps as we round 'em up drifting in."

Rod Duncan gulped and said, "She must have hoped you'd hesitate just long enough. I know you had to do it. I was there. But Jesus, I'm sure glad it wasn't me as had to gun a woman, pard!"

Longarm said, "I never did. Dolly must have been so used to the common courtesies accorded the unfair sex that he lost track of the fact I'd just told him I knew who he was."

"Who *he* was?" gasped the New Mexico lawman.

Longarm said, "Used to be a bearded lady, traveling with decent tent shows. Put on a less decent act whenever he, she, or it wasn't stopped. When I caught the act in Saint Lou a few years ago, he had half a man's suit and half a lady's gown on. You paid extra to go in the back and watch the he-she takes its duds off. I was as big a fool back then. Cost me four bits to discover he-she was just a soft-built boy. I wasn't interested in the girlish ways he could act for just a few dollars more. Reckon enough others were to finance more ambitious projects. Read a flyer later about this soft-built but hard-headed he-she marrying up with some rich mining man and robbing him blind on their honeymoon. Reckon old Dolly persuaded him she was saving it for her wedding night. Old Frenchy back there was the one true love of Dolly's life."

He finished reloading and put the derringer away as their back-up man stared goggle-eyed in the doorway and Duncan said, "Far be it from me to argue that the two of them weren't acting sort of strange. But what in thunderation was the *motive* for all this confusing shit?"

Longarm said, "I'll give you a copy of my report once I have everything tidied up complete. I got one more arrest to make first, and if you think I just felt silly gunning a lady in a red wig and pearls, you don't know the half of it!"

Chapter 19

Longarm had learned in his boyhood that things didn't always go as a body might plan them, and that sometimes it might be best to just play the cards a fickle fate dealt you.

He didn't want to stage a possibly awkward scene in front of a summer-school class. So he waited until he was sure Meg Campbell had come home from her job at the schoolhouse before he went calling.

He caught Trisha Myers in another big fib when the gal who came to the door turned out to be a stunningly beautiful brunette with deep blue eyes a man just wanted to drown in. But he figured it made more sense to show her his badge and identification.

She invited him right in and sat him down at her kitchen table to coffee and cake him as she allowed that Trisha had mentioned him, but had never told her he was a lawman.

He suspected why she sort of avoided his eyes when he asked what else the ash blonde might have said about him. The schoolmarm was blushing but composed herself as she murmured, "Just that the two of you were becoming . . . good friends. What's this all about, Deputy Long?"

He said, "My good friends call me Custis. They told me over at the hotel that Trisha didn't work there anymore. She wasn't at her own place, either. I finally found some old boys who'd been spitting and whittling in front of the tobacco shop when she'd ridden by, headed down the coach road to Santa Fe most likely. The wires ain't up yet, and I ain't sure I want her stopped in any case. Might that have been your mare she lit out on, Miss Meg?"

The schoolmarm sat down across from him, shaking her head firmly as she said, "My Pixie is right out back, if you'd care to see her."

Longarm said, "I'll take your word for it, ma'am. No lady capable of such fine marble cake would tell really dumb lies."

She met his eyes this time as she blazed, "See here, I've not a thing to hide from you or any other lawman! I haven't been the one in bed with an impossibly endowed man night after night, damn it!"

He didn't ask how disappointed she felt about that. He just smiled sheepishly and said, "She told me you were a dried-up old prune. But I ain't charging her with *that* big fib. I'm trying to determine how deep she was in more serious stuff. I turned to her to borrow your pony for me that night. I figured I might be able to confide in a waitress gal who didn't work for the *late* Queen Kirby. I figured wrong, and the two of them were playing me for a total sap until mighty recently."

Meg Campbell brightened and said, "So *that's* what it was! Did you say the *late* Queen Kirby? What happened to her?"

Longarm said, "You go first and I'll tell you the whole tangled tale from the beginning. What were you about to say something was?"

The brunette said, "Trisha boasted that whether you were willing to take her away from all this or not, she was going

177

to leave town on her own high-stepper, with money to start over in a real town. I guess I'm as nosy as I ought to be, and so I naturally kept after her about it. But all I got was that certain parties were willing to pay good money to learn harmless little secrets. Do you think she was telling Queen Kirby you'd been, you know, up in your hotel room?"

Longarm smiled thinly and replied, "I doubt Queen Kirby cared about my love life. That's all a matter of taste—literally, in Queen Kirby's case. But it's sort of soothing to know Trisha was only a dumb blonde after all. I doubt she'd ever be able to tell us more than we already know, and what's a little betrayal betwixt friends?"

The brunette poured some coffee for herself as she gently but firmly reminded Longarm he owed her a story.

Longarm washed down some cake and began. "Once upon a time there was this sort of odd couple, well-fixed for cash but on the dodge for having obtained the cash under many, many false pretenses. They came in their travels upon this bitty trail town, well-located but dying on the vine because it was located betwixt a haunted mesa and an Apache reservation. Being keen students of human nature, the couple I'll call Frenchy and Dolly saw folks were still unreasonably spooked by Indian troubles of the *past*. So it was possible to buy valuable property up this way cheap."

He took another bite and continued. "They did. One going business finances another, and so in no time at all Frenchy and Dolly became Queen Kirby and her boys. They naturally sent for other grifters to help them run their private town."

Meg Campbell protested, "They didn't own *all* of us. I'll have you know I was hired by the town council, not any card-house or parlor-house madam!"

He said soothingly, "I know. Almost half the town council is made up of more respectable old-timers. That's what was eating the greedy gent who was posing as a gal."

She gasped. "Good Lord! Queen Kirby was a *man*?"

Longarm said, "I reckon Trisha never told you because she never knew. He made a fairly convincing old gal, But that wasn't the crime that caused so much bother. There was a colonial governor back in the time of the real Queen Anne who liked to dress up like a fine lady, but he never dressed others up as Indians to spook folks even worse."

He saw he'd gotten ahead of himself again when she marveled, "Those Apache were dressed up silly too?"

He silenced her with a wave of his coffee cup and said, "Forget a heap of their unusual habits and you've still got greed. The natural laws of supply and demand raise real-estate values as a township gets more attractive to investors. They must have noticed how unwise it was to simply grab property the way they did down Lincoln County way. It was slicker when they grasped how Uncle John Chisum had wound up owning everything when the gunsmoke cleared, leaving the surviving property-holders demoralized and ready to sell out for a song. But as word got out about those Jicarilla being cleared to make room for progress, land values in these parts figured to go up, not down, and leave us not forget the rising price of beef back East. In sum, Queen Kirby's trail-town empire had finished expanding for the foreseeable future, unless they could make the future look different."

He sipped, put down the cup again, and said, "They sent out for more help. Some of them hardcase killers but mostly just adventurous saddle tramps. Only a small number of them had to be let in on their true plans. They didn't want to make it easy to add up the numbers, so they had some camping over in the canyonlands at first. That was a mistake they corrected as soon as they heard word was getting out to the real world about private armies gathering. They knew Governor Wallace and even the president who'd appointed him would be on the prod for another New Mexico dustup like that Lincoln County War. So they pulled them into town and enlisted them with the rest of their so-called Regulators before I ever got here."

"Regulators regulating what?" she demanded.

He said, "Apache, of course. Turns out no Jicarilla have really gone all that wild over the latest BIA nonsense. They likely figure Washington will reshuffle everybody back the way they were as soon as they get Victorio calmed down or buried. But everyone *else* with the hair and horseflesh they value was already braced for another Apache war before this county's effeminate answer to Uncle John Chisum decided to provide 'em with one. It was simple for Wes Jones, as Frenchy now called himself, to stage some Apache raids while pretending to be protecting all the white settlers from the savages. They didn't have to steal half as seriously as real raiders to scare the liver and lights out of folks. They didn't want to kill anyone capable of signing a bill of sale for some quick cash on the way to safer parts. So for all the dramatics, it was mostly hollow noise."

She poured him more coffee as she marveled, "Well, I never. But how much of this might Trisha have known, the two-faced thing?"

He grimaced and replied, "Not much. There was no need for hardly anyone they used to know what they were really up to. Trisha never came into the story before I came down from Colorado, by a devious route and a tad late. They'd known I was coming. We're still working on old pals they might have had on the BIA payroll, working for the railroad or whatever. Drifting grifters meet a lot of other shady sorts in their travels and a buck is always worth a hundred cents."

He sipped more coffee—she'd brewed it swell—and explained, "It was my getting here way later than expected that confounded them about me. I fear their first plan was to have me killed by Apache. I showed up not exactly as described after killing somebody else along the way. So, not wanting to waste a possibly valuable asset, Queen Kirby, or more likely the one you all knew as Wes Jones, came sneaking around, found Trisha in my room with me somewhere else, and made a quick deal with her."

Meg nodded and said, "She knew Wesley well. She said he was a generous tipper who was always nice to her. She seemed confused that he never asked her out after work."

Longarm said, "He had a steady sweetheart. But he persuaded the gal I'd been fool enough to confide in that they'd make it worth her while if she'd report every fool word I said to her to them!"

Meg fluttered her long lashes and murmured, "Heavens, I can see how foolish that might make you feel!"

He sighed and said, "I doubt they cared about my personal idiocy. I told Trisha who I really was. But then I told her I had no idea who I was really after or what might be going on. So they figured it was as easy and a heap safer to just hire me and have me where they could keep an eye on me as they got me to jump through hoops like a trained flea. They figured I'd tell Trisha when and if I commenced to suspect anything important, and they were right. I acted like a total sap, and even when I *did* start to get warm, I was still so far from the truth they'd have been better off letting me run down like a clock and head on home. Have you ever felt really *stupid,* Miss Meg?"

She reached across her table to pat the back of his big tanned hand and soothed, "It might have gone worse for us. If they were even partway onto you, and that two-faced Trisha hadn't convinced them you weren't onto *them*, they'd have killed you before you found out a thing and *then* where would we be?"

He put his own free hand atop hers—most men would have wanted to, and quietly replied, "You're doubtless right—and I reckon all's well as ends well. How come you asked where *we* would have wound up, Miss Meg? No offense, but I don't recall old Marshal Billy Vail putting *you* on the case with me."

The pretty schoolmarm looked away, cheeks flushed, as she murmured, "I guess I meant we'd have never been having this conversation, after Trisha had told me so much about you. I suppose you're in a hurry to get back to Denver, now that you've learned all there ever was to know about our dinky town?"

To which he could only reply, with a friendly squeeze, "I ain't so sure I've gotten to know everyone down this way as well as I'd like to. In any case I'll have to stick around long enough to tidy up a few loose ends and make sure law and order's been restored total."

She asked, in that case how many days, or hours, they might have to get to know one another better. When he suggested at least a good two days, she shyly suggested they'd best get *started* and so, what with one thing and another, it was over a week before Longarm got back to Denver, walking sort of funny.

Watch for

LONGARM AND THE BARBED WIRE BULLIES

190th in the bold LONGARM series
from Jove

Coming in October!

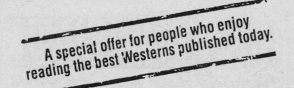

A special offer for people who enjoy reading the best Westerns published today.

WESTERNS!

NO OBLIGATION

Mail the coupon below

To start your subscription and receive 2 FREE WESTERNS, fill out the coupon below and mail it today. We'll send your first shipment which includes 2 FREE BOOKS as soon as we receive it.

Mail To: **True Value Home Subscription Services, Inc. P.O. Box 5235 120 Brighton Road, Clifton, New Jersey 07015-5235**

YES! I want to start reviewing the very best Westerns being published today. Send me my first shipment of 6 Westerns for me to preview FREE for 10 days. If I decide to keep them, I'll pay for just 4 of the books at the low subscriber price of $2.75 each; a total $11.00 (a $21.00 value). Then each month I'll receive the 6 newest and best Westerns to preview Free for 10 days. If I'm not satisfied I may return them within 10 days and owe nothing. Otherwise I'll be billed at the special low subscriber rate of $2.75 each; a total of $16.50 (at least a $21.00 value) and save $4.50 off the publishers price. There are never any shipping, handling or other hidden charges. I understand I am under no obligation to purchase any number of books and I can cancel my subscription at any time, no questions asked. In any case the 2 FREE books are mine to keep.

Name
_____

Street Address _____ Apt. No. _____

City _____ State _____ Zip Code _____

Telephone _____

Signature _____
(if under 18 parent or guardian must sign)

Terms and prices subject to change. Orders subject to acceptance by True Value Home Subscription Services, Inc.